SQUEAL

SQUEAL

A NOVEL

ENOCH ST. JOHN

ISBN: 0692201866

ISBN-13: 978-0692201862

Second Edition

Cover artwork by Miles Tsang

Cover design by Matt Musselman Design & PAPDesign

CONTENTS

SYNOPSIS

Tough-as-nails Jake Huntsman has been running a teen wilderness therapy camp for years. He's had to deal with juvenile delinquents of all sorts, yet the latest group of kids unnerves him a little.

Among the group are a few killers including an arsonist and a boy who drove a fellow classmate to suicide through cyber-bullying.

Still, Jake thinks the wilderness will set even this group of dangerous kids straight, and he'll ultimately end up doing what he's always done: successfully reform the wayward teens—or at least begin the process—with this character-building trip into forests he knows almost like the back of his hands.

But Jake quickly discovers he has more than troubled young adults to deal with as the group unexpectedly separates, and a murderous forest animal viciously takes them out one by one...

For you, my unborn son.

This little piggy went to market,
This little piggy stayed home,
This little piggy had roast beef,
This little piggy had none,
And this little piggy cried 'wee wee wee!' all the way home.
—Nursery Rhyme

ONE

RAZORBACK

This was a good idea.

Nate drew the moist, wild air into his lungs, cool breezes caressing his face and taking the edge off his residual anger. He knew that a trip to the hot springs would help alleviate the mounting clump of anxiety in his chest. No longer eating at him was his companion's insulting concern—questioning his ability to make an evening hike he had done since adolescence.

"You sure, bud?" Randy had asked when he proposed the hike, words steeped in hesitation spilling from his fat face. The good humor from their past hour of catching up melted away.

Randy's expression while he scrutinized Nate's leg was as clear as the color red, displayed for the pitiful and broken.

Nate took in a few breaths to calm himself—tolerating

people who interpreted the world in such a different way was part of the adjustment.

Despite Randy's misgivings, his old friend agreed to go, and after watching Randy shed his outer layers at the beginning of the trail, Nate was amazed he had managed to make the hike to the springs himself—he'd swelled more than just a few inches around the waist since he had last seen him. Randy had always been big, but not always so fat, his belly now peeking out from the bottom of his faded brown shirt with Santa-like proportions.

Nate suppressed disgust, trying not to look at the protruding belly and the pitiful, porky legs dragging it forward. A guy like Randy could never survive military training, much less war.

Nate couldn't believe that *this* man had been worried about whether or not he could make the hike, simply because of a prosthetic.

As they made their way through reaching limbs, the sharp reek of the hot springs soon greeted them, and they found themselves surrounded by lush, green, moss-laden forest, the moist reflective world illuminating the steaming pool.

Placing his flashlight aside, Randy plopped down at the rock-lined edge.

Nate sat and began working to remove the artificial appendage, then set it behind him.

He turned back toward the pool and lightly massaged his truncated limb.

Randy had already sent more than one glance its way, and Nate didn't blame him for being curious, but it was beginning to get on his nerves.

Nate moved into the water slowly, finding its depth.

The moment sent a thrill through him.

Standing on his own, he felt whole again, delighted by the vale of water restoring the balance between Randy and himself. Still built like a warrior, only the problems with his prosthetic kept him from deployment despite purposeful, powerful biceps and thighs, his arrow-shaped torso wrangled together by firm shoulders.

He took a moment to watch Randy see the truth, then moved on.

Nate closed his eyes and concentrated on the sounds around him: Randy shuffling around, the water flowing off the rocks in front of them like a leaky shower.

The hot water began working its usual magic, helping him unwind.

Nate inhaled deeply then exhaled, enjoying the feel of the heat against his skin and the summer air filling his lungs despite the stench.

Ignoring the spring's smell came easily, like ignoring PVC pipes some asshole left behind, positioned to make the flow of water more functional; the world out here could afford such a trivial encroachment with its expansive beauty.

Suddenly, Nate's serenity broke, and he opened his eyes to find the source of the interruption, catching Randy's gaze on him.

He resented the sympathy he saw looking back.

So far, Randy didn't have the balls to directly ask him about his time at war, or even his treatments and the grueling rehabilitation program.

"Hey, I'm really glad you could make it back up here again—I mean, back home and all," Randy said brightly, surprising Nate with his tact.

"You know my leg is not an embarrassment," Nate said flatly.

"No, I just meant..."

"Randy, relax. It sucked, but with all the work I put in, I can do anything."

"I just thought it was a sore subject, being so recent and all."

"Nah. Honestly, it's a point of pride in my unit. I mean, I passed my PFTs, I'm back to where I can run, swim, shoot my gun and everything," Nate said, smiling, happy to explain. He missed the daily pride he used to feel for his injury.

"Well, why did you get shit-canned?" Randy said, deflating him for a brief moment.

"See, the problem is no knee, so I can't do *everything*,

but anything a normal guy would do—or a fat turd like you."

Randy burst into laughter. Then he crushed the blue beer can between his sausage fingers and tossed it high in the air behind him, quickly pulling up the tab of another.

Nate stared at the carelessly discarded can.

Randy was on his third beer, but had the courtesy to at least bring two six-packs with him since he had the tendency to kill a pack himself pretty quickly. Still, Randy didn't have the decency or awareness to bring some kind of trash bag to clean up after himself.

Nate hated him again—his myopic perspective, and even that faded John Deere trucker cap he still wore. He resented his long, greasy-looking dirty blond hair, the hair he let sprout randomly from his body, the unkempt beard and mustache, and especially the wretched contentment he wore on his face.

Nate didn't have a hair in sight on his torso; he kept himself groomed and shaved at home—it was the appropriate thing to do.

Randy grinned widely despite Nate's pointed stare, looking like a giant, mischievous little boy.

"Sorry, man—I'll take care of it. I was just fuckin' with you."

Randy scurried over to the can, snatched it up, then waddled over to the pile of belongings he had made, opened his backpack and dropped it in.

Nate relaxed and grinned back at him; his old friend had grown up a bit.

Randy wasn't a bad guy—not worse than anyone else—and had been his best friend since elementary school when Randy scared off a group of boys about to gang up on him. No one was happier to see Nate when he returned from his trips to Afghanistan, Iraq, or Yemen, and no one was happier his service was over now—although it took half his leg getting blown clean away to do it.

Like the rest of the world, Nate sort of chopped things up to make them tolerable. Randy was relatively honest—or at least a bad liar—and loyal; so, taken in parts, he was bearable, and their friendship, worthwhile.

"You still have that Ford Vick?" Nate asked.

Randy smiled appreciatively. "Still safe and sound in my dad's old trailer. Probably hasn't moved since you first left."

"So you haven't done anything to it?"

"I mean, I took the oil out."

"You lazy shit," Nate said lightly, grinning at him.

"I got plans," Randy said, smiling back. "Hey, remember when..." he began, when a loud snap interrupted him.

They both froze.

Then Nate relaxed. "Branch—just an old tree giving up," he said knowingly.

A large, bubbling gurgle erupted from the water.

"Did you just fart?" Nate asked. "Not that I could tell the difference with the smell around here."

Randy chuckled. "The springs, man," he said, dingy teeth gleaming under Nate's flashlight.

"You sure? I know you fart when you get nervous." Nate examined his friend's face.

Another crackle in the brush changed Randy's expression, and Nate saw clearly that Randy was afraid.

"You look scared. What're you scared of?"

"I ain't scared, man—nothin' out here to be afraid of. I killed every type of thing that lives up here."

But Nate was well aware how the night played on the mind, shadows and sounds suggesting a myriad of possibilities.

Randy shook his head. "I've hunted for years. I'm more afraid of you than anything I'll find out here."

Randy again reached over to his pile and peeked open his backpack, flashing Nate his gun. "You ain't the only one who can wield one of these," he said.

"You think that pistol could stop the *giant* boar?" Nate said, deliberately affecting a sinister tone.

Randy looked away. "I wish we still had those hairy little pig shits out here. Might as well hunt at a farm—just scared hogs with bad teeth and a pimp coat. My cousin shot one like fifteen years ago and still won't stop talking about it. Weighed about three hundred pounds."

"You know I don't mean some three-hundred-pound

swine. I'm talkin' about the one that weighs about half a ton, the one over a thousand pounds. You think it might come here tonight, don't you? Big old beast coming at you all bristles and tusks, all huge and stinky and gray like some rabid elephant."

Nate giggled at his friend's obvious discomfort as he writhed, unable to meet his eye.

"Oh shit, Nate—nobody even talks about monster boars anymore with the regular ones nearly all gone," Randy said, then dipped underwater, holding himself below the surface for about half a minute. Then he sprang up, sucking and slurping air with a proud look on his face. "Pretty good, huh?"

"Yeah. Amazing." Nate rolled his eyes.

Randy gave him a wry grin, then turned to reach for another beer can.

Nate took the opportunity to slip behind him, unleashing a snarling, hog-like grunt, startling Randy. Randy hopped a few inches up, barking out a childlike scream, then landed with a plop.

The unmistakable sound of a low but lengthy, almost musical fart escaped his friend.

Nate erupted into laughter and fell back into the pool.

"Hell, I need to take a shit now," Randy said, grinning at him. "I'll be right back."

Randy pulled himself upright and over the smooth rock like a baby learning to walk, then hurried away with his flashlight, disappearing into the darkness, his heavy footsteps fading as he became a mere beam of light getting smaller and smaller.

The quietude brought into sharp focus the sounds of the calm night: grasshoppers chirping, wind and small animals, rustling leaves, the smell of pines facing off against the sulfurous spring.

Nate hoped Randy had gone far enough that the smell of the forest still reigned over anything else about to leave his body.

"Hope everything comes out okay," Nate shouted into the wooded darkness, lifting his head a bit as if the action would help his voice go further.

The movement made the night sky catch his eye, and he was struck by how much the stars still comforted him, nodding at him like old comrades, and how the view of the sky made possible by the vast nothingness of a desert war was achieved here by simple elevation.

Before long, Nate had lost track of time, and began to worry. He knew it could have been just a few minutes, but he felt a familiar dread come over him, followed by the stirrings of a panic attack. The visceral, full body overreaction was a common side effect among his peers, and he had become much better at settling himself.

He took in a deep breath, thinking only of the air filling his lungs, then released it.

Then a monstrous grunt echoed through the night,

tearing him from his meditation, followed by the horrified scream of a man in mortal danger.

Shit, I was just messing around! he thought, but he recognized the animal behind the hair-raising snorting and chomping now weaving in and out of rippling cries for help that he could not get a bearing on.

Another scream helped him lock in on their location.

"I'm coming!" he shouted, holding back panic. "Hang on!"

He began attaching his prosthetic as fast as he could.

Once in place, he got up, readying his knife for the beast should it come crashing through the dark.

Welcome adrenaline rushed through him as he ran, making him feel alive, redeployed. He could take on the horrid beast, prosthetic leg and all, with just his knife and brains.

"No! Oh god, why!" Randy shouted as Nate slashed through the forest toward the sound of his friend's tortured cries. "Nate!"

"I'm coming!"

Nate hoped his voice could help his friend hold on, give him something tangible to grab on to.

The fake leg deftly pounded the ground, but in a flash, Nate found himself flat on his face.

He began peeling himself from the forest floor, stupefied.

Had he not put the leg on properly? Did he get caught by a root?

Nate double-checked his leg, then stood slowly, frustration growing to anger at the hindrance, at the stub pretending to be his leg. For all the denial since the very beginning that a prosthetic hampered him, for the first time since getting it, he cried out in anger, tasting helplessness at last.

Then the smell of iron in the air, as blood met it, hit his nose—the familiar stench of battle, flesh, and death.

"I'm almost there!" he shouted, no longer able to gauge the distance with the sudden silence. *Just hang on...*

Then Nate heard the massive animal running, pounding the forest floor.

Was it preparing for a second strike? Or frightened away by his fallen flashlight?

As Nate grabbed for the light, he realized it wasn't his, but Randy's. He turned to search the area, and found Randy just behind him, and it dawned on him that it was Randy's body that had tripped him—the blood on his prosthetic confirmed it.

There his old friend lay, splayed, the last of the light leaving disbelieving eyes. Blood leaked from exposed veins, gutted by the terrible animal's tusks.

"Oh, Randy," Nate heard himself say as he sank to his knees, immersing himself in Randy's blood.

Then he felt something rising in him, and unsure if it

was vomit or hysteria, he turned away from the now unseeing eyes of his oldest friend toward the darkness of the forest. He concentrated on his breath again, his awareness of the action easing him.

He didn't have the luxury of time to mourn; he needed to get away. But which way?

Soon, he heard the charging feet of the horrible animal, the snapping click of the twisted tusks, then a sharp, guttural squeal.

TWO

PIGS IN A BLANKET

Please note: an inspection of all items will take place before entry into the van.

NO SMUGGLING.

All your belongings and your person will be searched multiple times.

Melanie Petrova giggled when she saw the notice with her letter of acceptance to the WISH summer cycle.

Your person. Who really used this phrase?

Melanie imagined a helper with her—a dwarf perhaps —and him getting searched on her behalf, shrugging as he got patted down, resigned eyes on her.

How hard would the inspectors look, really?

When the day came, she would enter the van with only the basics as mandated as far as the camp leaders were concerned: underwear and toiletries, wearing a plain, long-sleeved shirt and a pair of shorts since the camp would issue their clothing.

The camp allowed a brush for basic upkeep, but no makeup—although she didn't care about the makeup ban; nothing mattered as much as her personal first aid kit.

The notice was clear about sharp objects and illegal substances: none allowed, but no one could disagree that she needed a small box of tampons, so in one of those cylindrical pieces, she hid a tiny, white rock, and her compact glass one-hitter. In another, a razor, carefully cushioned with a few tabs of acid.

Please eat before your pickup time, as the only snacks allowed are the ones in the backpack issued to you, and you will not want to deplete those too quickly.

When she got to the next section, Melanie almost giggled again, near hysteria:

Entertainment items will be considered on a case-by-case basis.

What sort of things had people brought in the past that qualified as an entertainment item? An iPod? A yo-yo? A dildo? The letter made it quite clear no such objects would be approved.

Fear descended on her as she wondered what kind of people she would be stuck with for three weeks to warrant such strict security in the ride to the hiking site.

The letter had given her no idea of what the other kids were like, what they had done.

She figured since none of them knew anything about each other, they would probably all be on guard as they sat side by side in the van, unsure what the person next to, behind, or in front of them was capable of.

They would know just one thing: they were all bad.

———

"I USUALLY GET a pair of shoes for that," Narine said to the butch-looking woman who patted her down one last time before she got in the van.

Despite all the other open rows, she headed for the first row of seats which held the only other occupant, and immediately hated the girl sitting there.

"What are you supposed to be?" she said to the distracted-looking blonde as she sat next to her.

The girl seemed shocked and confused, jolted out of her daydream. Her mouth moved like a fish as she struggled for words.

Narine decided to end her struggle. "Just kidding. I'm Narine."

"Melanie," the girl replied, extending her hand, and Narine shook it with her fingers, flashing her a quick, phony smile.

She sniffed out quickly how pathetic and frail the girl was, and Narine hated weaklings.

She wondered how the hell the girl got under her skin, beyond being so pitiful.

Damn her, it had to be that blond hair of hers; it looked so natural—a shade Narine dreamed of and could never get.

And were her eyes blue, too? And not just any blue; a gorgeous blue—like the ocean in her friend's mom's pictures from her trip to Jamaica, not knowing that while she was gone with her daughter, Narine had the opportunity to fuck her husband and get a breathtaking necklace out of the deal for her silence.

Ugh. What a lucky, bony bitch.

Narine turned away and held her hands out in front of her.

She had her nails done with shellac nail polish a few days before, so her fingernails and toenails would look great for at least two weeks. She had to go with a more 'natural' polish since the camp was so damned strict, and went with a kind of peachy pink, like the inside of a conch shell she had seen in her friend's home from that trip to Jamaica.

When Narine saw the camp list, it almost made her mad, but she was slightly amused by it. But who did they think they were? No makeup? No perfume? What the hell? Who could it possibly harm? It wasn't like she could stab someone with mascara or bludgeon them to death with some lipstick.

They thought they were so smart. Well, if they were so smart, how come they didn't find her lip gloss hidden underneath her deodorant stick?

And they certainly didn't pick up that the body lotion she totally needed for her 'special' super-dry skin had some makeup mixed in. Fuck them—she would look glowy at least.

She couldn't find a way to smuggle in her root touchup items, but there was no way anyone would catch her not looking pretty.

And no phones? Were they serious?

She had tried to smuggle in her smart phone, but her mom had found it hiding in her bra.

Her mother looked so smug seeing her stripped down.

Jealous cow. Didn't she know all she had to do was bleach her own thick, dark hair and brighten up her eyes with…anything really, and she could at least look half as good as her daughter? And if only she wore more flattering clothes.

No wonder her father had a girlfriend. Who wanted to come home to a plain old boring woman like that?

Narine knew several of the men who bought things for her had wives too. She noticed the wedding rings on some of their fingers, didn't miss the casual comment about their 'significant other' being off on a short weekend trip, and she always imagined their wives looking like her mom:

little to no makeup, dull, drab hair and eyes too sincere and sad to be sexy.

Those men probably wished they had married a girl like her instead, and she felt sorry for them—stuck with such stupid, ugly heifers in sexless, un-stimulating relationships.

The men treated her so well—bought her anything she wanted, and all she had to do was lie there, or sneak into a bathroom stall with them and suck on them for a few minutes.

In no time, she had a new Louis Vuitton handbag, or a pair of Louboutin shoes.

She had once spent a week in the company of one man, and ended up getting all the things from the list she had made the week before: a spa day at a ritzy new place in Beverly Hills, her hair done at a trendy salon, more MAC makeup, and that cute pink and black Betsy Johnson dress she had seen in a window.

She always got what she wanted, whether or not her parents got it for her or agreed she could have it.

How they could still dare to open their mouths and refer to her as a child was beyond her; she was clearly a woman—her body said it quite loudly.

She looked no different from the girls in the catalogues —everyone said she should be a model; in fact, she didn't look much different from the girl she had once caught her father with—his current girlfriend. The girl was maybe five years older than her, but her chest was smaller, and her waist, not as small.

Narine knew if she ever decided to get married, she would never end up all ugly and pathetic like her mother.

God, she wished the hag would get a life.

———

CHILDREN ARE ONLY *as dangerous as they are hurt,* Jake thought every time a kid entered his van, and all he could think about was the offense that brought them to where they were now: heading out for the wilderness retreat he had christened WISH at its inception four years ago.

Narine and Melanie were soon joined by the boys— the small, redheaded one joining the girls in the first row, the largest one settling behind them with the Asian boy, and the black kid getting in last, joining the Hispanic girl in the back row.

Jake's hired muscle sat behind them with all the bags, ready to intervene at a moment's notice.

After closing them in, Jake hopped in the driver's seat, ignoring his assistant in the passenger's seat whose eyes were closed, although he was clearly not taking a nap.

He was probably praying.

Individually, Jake didn't find the teenagers intimidating himself—kids like these got humbled by the unknowns of the wilderness in a jiffy; it happened every cycle without fail. As long as their families had enough money to afford this treatment program, he had no doubt these kids knew enough to realize the luxuries they had left behind. No more pampering and negotiating, no more slaps on the wrist. Completely wrestled away from the familiar, 'incorrigible' kids like these learned to change quickly.

Jake once had a group of ten where the biggest crime among the misfits was theft. That group consisted of two kleptomaniacs, three alcoholics, and two potheads. Others had simply been antisocial, or consistently got bad grades, but they were generally mild troubled teens.

But the group of kids this cycle unnerved him a bit— among them, an arsonist, an armed robber, and a pathological liar who drove a fellow classmate to suicide.

Still, no matter how bad the kids were as a group, the wilderness would set them straight—at least, most of them —and they would return home closer to being the little angel their parents thought they were or could be, on their way to rehabilitation.

Jake even expected letters of gratitude from both parents and kids for changing their lives, about how much they owed him for such an awesome, gratifying experience.

Six hours into the drive, they arrived at the last turn.

The popping of branches, and the crunch of tires on loose dirt woke few of the napping, jet-lagged teens, others jolting awake at the sudden bouncing through uneven terrain.

He stopped the van and ordered everyone out.

His burly hired hand dumped the backpacks out of the back, then got in the driver's seat and drove off.

Jake tried not to smile at some of the mouths dropping open as the van peeled off.

"All right, line up toward the pathway and spread out," he ordered, sending his assistant, Eric, ahead of them. "This is our first exercise in teamwork. We will pass the packs down the line toward Mr. Green, and he will check them one final time and assign them to you, understood?"

The young, black kid, Joe, smiled as he nodded.

"I'm glad you're so happy about it," Jake said. "Now start tossing them."

The kid's grin disappeared as he obeyed.

Joe handed the pack to Bluto, the huge boy next to him, who then passed it on.

All went smoothly until the second to last bag, which Bluto swatted back at Joe, hitting him, and knocking him almost off his feet.

Joe immediately looked at Jake for a response, and Jake stalked up to Bluto, grabbed him by the wrist, and then twisted it in a hold that brought him to his knees.

He bent to the large boy's ear and whispered:

"Not out here, you little fuck."

Bluto winced as he twisted his wrist again, but he made no sound.

"Jake," he heard Eric say gently.

Jake loosened his grip on the boy's wrist, but kept hold of it so he could hoist him to his feet.

He stepped back and addressed the startled group.

"Let's get a few things straight," he said. He pointed at Eric without looking at him. "That's my assistant, Eric Green. My name is Jacob Scott Huntsman, and to many of you, I'm just some asshole who has to take you camping. But this is not a camping trip, as you will find out quickly. The reason I drove you six hours off-trail down a crappy dirt road, far away from service centers or any hope of reaching anything you know, is because on this trip, you will have nothing but me and each other to rely on. Even if you managed to get a phone this far, it won't help you. Any games you play out here will be dangerous—there are real threats. This is the wild, and I am your leader, your hope, your Higher Power. Now let's get going."

———

THE HOH RAINFOREST spoke for itself.

The open view provided at the start of the hike was quickly snatched away as they entered it, swallowing them whole like the mouth of a great beast.

The entrance Jake chose had a dense canopy, creating

the perfect dramatic beginning to his process—the moss, a glorious emerald, trees stabbing through the rippling green ceiling.

A conveniently located group of trees set in line by a nursery log greeted the group at the first bend, trunks shredded by immense bear claw marks.

The canopy seemed only to grant beams of light permission to break in—one such beam almost directly leading the eye to the clawed trees.

Jake liked to watch the kids as they took that first turn and he explained the claw marks; the obvious presence of a bear made them all wary. But this time around, one kid seemed not to be affected at all, like he had missed it.

Another kid asked where they would take their showers or how long the food issued to them in their backpacks could possibly last them, and Jake took great delight in letting them all know just how much they would be roughing it.

He took them away from safer pathways to walk them through grabbing branches, past views of sharp drop-offs.

The hike also gave Jake a better opportunity to assess each teen, even as his mouth went on about using springs and streams, about trapping animals and spitfires.

Thirty minutes to an hour in, and he could already tell the first layer of defense for some had been peeled away, as the kids seemed to finally open their eyes to the reality of the harsh environment.

With all the signs of regular civilization having dropped away to bushes and branches, roots and curious, wooded animals, they had surely begun to feel a vulnerability they had never felt before.

A few held fast to their armor or otherwise remained impassive, including Bluto. He was bigger than all of them —even Jake by an inch or so in height, and definitely in breadth. The boy came in over six feet, and well over two hundred pounds, and had entered the van with a surly look on his face—perhaps an attempt to ward off anyone who might think to provoke him, as if his size might not be enough.

But once Jake put him in his place after that stunt he pulled with Joe, Bluto knew who was boss—at least, for now.

The other kid who sent up a red flag for him was David Zhang. Jake wondered how the boy had managed to take the claw marks in stride—his private investigator hadn't pulled up anything that would shed light on this boy's valor.

The first thing Jake needed to know when he ran the background checks was whether prospective juveniles had any physical problems, since kids with medical problems were not allowed; he couldn't be responsible for some kid forgetting to take, losing, or running out of their asthma medicine—it was enough dealing with their emotional and psychological problems.

Once cleared physically, his investigators found out their patterns, what trouble they got into at school. What their friends and acquaintances made of them—especially since parents almost always tried to soften their kid's problems and crimes in his interviews with them.

It rarely failed—whatever their kid was guilty of, the parents downplayed it, tried to make it seem like the crime or vice had nothing to do with who their kid really was. That theirs was a good kid—he/she just got caught up in the wrong crowd. It was always someone else's fault.

One exception this time around was the thin, sad girl with the Russian father—Melanie. The man had told Jake outright that his daughter was a whore, and she wasn't coming back into his house until she behaved like a lady. Jake had to suppress a chuckle—his camp may have worked miracles in the past, but it was no etiquette school. Still, he could tell she wouldn't really pose a problem to the other kids—her issues endangered only her.

Jake's main concern was the kids who might harm others one way or another—those were the ones he had to watch extra carefully. Like that redheaded kid when it came to fire.

The rest of the teens seemed manageable, but Jake was well aware how people sometimes changed in the presence of others like themselves or their opposite, for better or worse.

He sure hoped he was right in his original assessment

of having to be extra vigilant with only two of the brats; looking out for more than that could get taxing.

If he made it through this group, his camp's profile would be raised, and with his reputation skyrocketing, he would get more grants and contracts, and WISH would live on.

THREE

PEARLS BEFORE SWINE

The fire was beautiful.

Joe had never thought that way about fire before, but here at night, deep in the forest with eight strangers—six of them kids like him, and two adult camp leaders—it commanded attention.

The fire seemed to dance, sparks highlighting the graceful flickering of yellow-orange flames. It bathed his dark brown skin with a sort of golden light.

Joe figured he was probably the youngest of the pack, even though he knew he didn't look it.

He had just turned thirteen the day before, but he didn't tell anyone about his birthday as they all headed to the forest in the van in silence.

Like everyone else probably did, he had taken a quick look at who else was there, what the people he would be spending a few weeks with looked like.

It wasn't physically obvious to him what anyone had done to earn a spot here at the wilderness retreat, to have to wear a bright yellow T-shirt with the word WISH on the front, "Wilderness Intervention for Solutions and Healing" on the back in blue lettering. He was grateful no one but themselves would see each other in the humiliating gear.

The camp leader yapped on about his background, then his ideals and why they were here, as well as what he hoped they would get out of the experience, but Joe was busy checking out the other youngsters having to listen to this crap and be out here in the wilderness on punishment now that they had a moment.

"This is not a boot camp," Mr. Huntsman said. "I'm not here to be your drill sergeant and teach you how to do fifty push-ups in one-minute; that's not the kind of discipline this camp is interested in."

Joe's eyes kept going to the Mexican-looking girl he sat next to on the van, and who had briefly smiled at him in greeting. If he had to guess, he would say she was fourteen or fifteen, maybe.

"This retreat is about learning to value people—their lives, and loved ones they may have in them. Their feelings, their thoughts, their hard work..."

Next to her sat the sort of pretty girl, one he knew wasn't white, but tried to make herself look like she was. She had already made the camp shirt look better—her boobs swelling out of it in a distracting way, especially since the rest of her body was so slim. Her hair was an obvious dyed blond—an unnatural shade with dark roots. She wore contacts, too—he could tell; he had a cousin who wore them, experimenting with blue ones here, green ones there. Despite the huge difference in shade between the two girls—his cousin, almost dark as midnight, this girl, a tan color people usually called olive, although he never understood why since he had only seen black and green ones—the contacts looked just as fake. This girl was probably fifteen or sixteen at least. He wondered why she was here—she came across pretty rich, and didn't people like them buy their way out of everything? Even this?

"You will learn to focus and be self-sufficient, yet work together. How to take control of your lives. You'll learn about different kinds of strengths, and yes, even compassion."

Joe glanced over at the Asian boy staring downward and couldn't guess a single reason why he would be here. He, like the rest of them, had stayed pretty quiet during the arduous hike.

"Don't be surprised if you find yourself having made lifelong friends on this retreat..."

Someone snickered, but as he looked around, Joe couldn't tell from whom it had come.

"You'll have to rely on each other, and you'll end up

learning a lot about yourself, as well as working with other people."

Joe briefly glanced at the giant white guy who hit him with the bag, then looked down when he looked back.

"Keep in mind—although I know we have an expert among us, I'll start the fires out here unless otherwise instructed."

This caught Joe's attention, and he looked around to see who the expert could be. It seemed to him the leader took great pains not to glance in this person's direction, but one quick look around and Joe figured it out—only one other person was watching the fire the way he probably had been earlier: with reverence.

It was a small, pale, redheaded kid with glasses.

"Believe it or not, most of what we need is in here," Mr. Huntsman said, pointing two thumbs toward the backpack behind him as he sat on a log facing them instead of around the fire with them.

Despite the leader's backpack being much larger than the ones he had issued them, Joe wondered how what they needed for three weeks could possibly fit.

Then he lost interest and went back to scrutinizing the other kids, beginning with the super-skinny white chick on his right. Skin pale as the moon, large blue eyes, short, naturally blond-looking hair with a streak of purple, she looked clean, but something was off about her; she had a kind of absence to her that reminded him of strung out girls in his neighborhood. Plus, she looked like she was on crack the way her skin clung to her bones. Maybe that's why she was here.

"Now, I've hiked this area about a hundred times—before I even started this wilderness program—and I cannot remind you enough: do not eat anything from the bushes, no matter how edible it looks. There are a good number of poisonous berries out there, but we'll be able to find and make safe food. You have enough nutrition for about three days right now in your backpacks, but you'll be surprised what you can do with your own two hands."

Joe's eyes came back around to the sad-looking Mexican girl. He wondered why she looked so bummed, what she could have done. All the rest looked like they had something lurking underneath, so he wouldn't be surprised by any of their offenses, but he couldn't imagine what this girl could be guilty of.

"Remember this, kids, no matter how bad you think you are, there is still redemption. You're here because someone loves you—your mom, your dad, your grandmother. Each and every one of you has someone on your side, and you will find that to be one of the great things in life: having someone looking out for you. You have your whole life ahead of you, and you're lucky you got to this place early—no one's gonna hold any of the stuff you did before against you.

"We're gonna be a team out here, and learn to trust

people, and how good it is to have someone to lean on. How much stronger we are than our bad luck, the circumstances we were born into, the bad choices we made."

Joe felt the leader's eyes on him so he kept his eyes averted.

Then the leader said:

"Part of our bonding will be full disclosure. Everyone here will give their name, and talk about why they think they're here. Don't worry, I won't violate your trust and tell everyone what you were submitted for; I'll leave it up to you to interpret or decide how much to say right now. But do know, I'll know if you're lying. Let's start with you, Narine." Mr. Huntsman looked over at the pretty, olive-skinned girl.

Narine rolled her temporarily blue eyes.

"Narine Abajian, and I'm here because my mom hates that I'm prettier than her. She can't deal with me being in her face every day while she gets older and wrinklier."

Narine folded slim arms over her protruding chest, sapphire eyes looking off to the side.

Joe didn't miss the look on Mr. Huntsman's face. Even without it, it was obvious the girl was lying—each of them was there because of something concrete, something that, had they been old enough, they could have gotten real jail time for. Instead, to avoid charges that would have put them in juvenile detention or worse, they had all agreed to the completion of this three-week wilderness camp.

"I'll start," the Mexican girl said, and Joe's ears pricked up. She wasn't super pretty or anything, and definitely wasn't skinny, but he was interested. She had thick, shiny black hair currently in a long braid, but it was her eyes that entranced him, made him want to know more about her. Maybe even help her in some way—although she looked like she could probably handle herself if push came to shove; despite the soft look of her, he could see she was tough.

Joe caught a flash of something shimmering underneath one of her eyes, like the remains of a teardrop from having wiped her hand across it, smearing it instead of erasing it.

Mr. Huntsman smiled, obviously appreciating the girl's willing participation.

"Go ahead, Luz: full name, age, where you're from, and then why you think you're here. We'll come back to you, Narine."

Narine rolled her eyes again, arms still folded, then looked away.

Luz let out a breath.

The shimmery path underneath her eye winked in the firelight.

"I'm Maria Velasquez, but everyone calls me Luz. I'm from San Diego, I'm fourteen, and I'm here because my grandmother took up a church collection to help pay for this camp because she didn't want to see me die like a gang-banger." She paused. "She doesn't like that I've been seeing this guy who's in a gang."

And then she stopped again, in a way that made Joe think there was more to say, but she decided not to.

Jake Huntsman, thirty-four, ex-marine, didn't push her, probably happy she willingly participated.

Joe smiled to himself, surprised he had registered some of the leader's bio.

"Looks like you're ready to go next, Joe," Mr. Huntsman said, his voice strong and authoritative.

Joe felt compelled to do his bidding.

His voice had finally stopped cracking—crossing over from a boyish tone to a more manly one—and it had been consistently masculine for the past few months, making him feel a bit more confident.

Still, he cleared his throat just in case.

"I'm Joe Lambert, thirteen, and I was in a robbery. My friends had me hold down the store owner while they robbed the place. I...I honestly didn't know what was going down."

"Yeah, right," he heard, then figured out it had come from the bully.

He regretted his last words, wondering if it made him look weak; he didn't want to look weak out here.

He suddenly became aware of everyone checking him out then.

He had noticed people doing that to him lately, while he was horsing around with friends. Earlier in the summer, shirtless due to the heat, he realized older girls and women looked at him a certain way. He figured they probably thought he was older due to his body size and type—he had grown a lot quickly, and suddenly had muscles cut in his arms, his chest, his stomach. People probably looked at him and assumed he could take down anyone, and it was probably what his friends thought when they gave him his unexpected task; he had even surprised himself with the results.

The mere fact of him speaking seemed to make the bully mad, because he then threw him a mean look before deciding to go next.

"Well, I'm Chris Hansen, but people call me Bluto. I'm fifteen, and I smash little bitches."

He punched his fist into his palm for emphasis, and his glittery black eyes looked into Joe's as if daring him.

Joe thought Bluto's nickname misplaced—the only Bluto he knew was the guy from *Popeye*, and the two maybe had size in common, but this boy didn't have the muscles his cartoon namesake had.

"Melanie?" Mr. Huntsman's voice interrupted the silent challenge.

The skinny blond girl next to Joe looked up, and it took her a few seconds to speak.

"Melanie Petrova," she began.

She had an accent—European.

Joe wondered where she was from and how she had come all the way to America to end up here.

"Fifteen. San Francisco."

And then, without warning, she started crying softly.

"Kicked out of home—stripper," she managed to say through her fingers.

"Melanie, Melanie, Melanie," Bluto began in what Joe recognized as a falsely gentle, sympathetic voice. "Why don't you tell the whole truth? We're all friends here."

Melanie looked at him as if she believed him.

No way she could be that gullible, Joe thought.

"I mean, *I* know why you're really here," Bluto continued, "I can see it all over you—why a girl like you is wearing such an ugly, long-sleeved shirt underneath this even uglier camp shirt. I mean, sure, it's not exactly warm out here, but you're hiding something, ain't you, Melanie? Besides probably a few cuts here and there?"

And then, in a surprisingly good tenor voice he started singing:

"I bet I can figure out Melanie's crime. Let me see...a rock or a dime?"

"Okay, Bluto, that's enough," the camp leader's

assistant said, surprising Joe since he had forgotten he was there.

Joe vaguely remembered him being present on the van ride sitting shotgun, asking Mr. Huntsman questions here and there, talking about things Joe wasn't interested in overhearing.

Joe figured Eric was around the same age as Mr. Huntsman—perhaps a little younger. In any case, Eric looked like a man-baby in a way—his body that of a man, his face like a young boy's. He had amazingly childlike blue eyes with golden eyelashes matching his short, blond hair. He wasn't very tall, but he was stocky and muscular.

Mr. Huntsman let Eric talk about himself for a bit once they set up camp, and after giving his bio, he had said:

"And let me just say one thing: whether you know it or not, God loves each and every one of you and has already forgiven you your past transgressions. Don't be afraid to pray for his guidance. If you need any help getting started, just let me know."

Joe remembered registering kind-looking eyes, and that Eric sounded like he meant every word. Joe trusted him immediately—not that Mr. Huntsman didn't strike him as kind or genuine—he had simply carved himself out as a leader, and didn't seem as approachable as Eric. But Joe had no doubt Mr. Huntsman knew what he was doing.

"You know this shit won't save you, Mel, you're already dead. Joe, how long do crack hoes last?"

Bluto was clearly enjoying himself.

Joe ignored the question.

Melanie's crying had already intensified at Bluto's sudden attack, and after he spat "tweaker" in her direction following Eric's reproach, Melanie sprang up and ran off into the forest.

"Shit," Mr. Huntsman said as he got up to follow her, leaving his heavy-looking backpack behind.

Joe giggled at Eric's slightly offended-looking face at the leader's word choice, then watched the chase with interest.

For such a scrawny thing, Melanie was shockingly fast, and disappeared long before Mr. Huntsman could reach her.

FOUR

HAM-HANDED

Such a crappy fucker, Melanie thought as she sat on a mound of leaves packed up against a tree.

Why would he say such a thing? Men were usually so nice to her.

Maybe that was the problem—the big one, he was still a boy. If he had seen her at work and he was a real man, he would treat her like the others. Give her money just for existing. Tell her sweet things.

Melanie stilled as she heard the camp leader run past her.

It would be almost impossible for him to track her down before she wanted to be found—she had a knack for disappearing.

She relaxed again, confident she was in the clear as the leader's voice faded away, calling her name.

She became upset again at the unexpected attack.

How did he know? How did the fat one know about her cutting? She had taken care to hide her arms. Why would he think that about her?

She lifted her left sleeve and felt the tiny scars lining her limb, trying to remember what they looked like in the light. She tried to guess how many were there now, like candy in a jar.

There must've been more than fifty—after counting one side of her forearm alone she reached eighteen before stopping.

She had stifled her cries so the counsellor wouldn't detect her, but now that he seemed far enough away, she indulged in her emotion.

Then she remembered she had prepared well for this trip.

Just as she had suspected, as a female, and a child according to law, the search wasn't conducted thoroughly; vital areas had been skipped.

She pulled out a rock of crystal meth and the tiny lighter she managed to sneak in. She didn't realize how much she was shaking, and after taking one steady drag, the rock popped out of the pipe, then slipped through her clumsy fingers when she tried to catch it, falling into the dark forest. She frantically looked around for it using her now almost useless lighter as a torch, then quickly snuffed out the light when she thought she heard a sound.

She sat still, listening.

It wasn't the camp leader calling her name.

It could have been anything, really—it was a forest after all. A possum, perhaps a lizard, or a harmless raccoon.

She relaxed.

How could she have dropped the precious rock? She had always been so good with her hands. Lately, she had been wishing she had used them more for what she liked to do, rather than what she had to do for money.

She remembered showing her dad her first real painting, so proud after so many first drafts, happily gifting it to him. He appeared to study it for a few moments, then walked out to their back porch and promptly set it on fire.

As she stood there, frozen, he told her there was no future in being an artist.

"Name one painter alive who is rich," he had said. "One single painter who made a fortune based off of their stupid sketches. Who came from nothing and is now living with a fortune from that. Go ahead. And if you manage to do that, name another."

Of course she hadn't been able to name any she hadn't really studied the subject yet. She knew a lot of famous painters had died poor, and her father probably knew that too.

Still, she had been able to work on other things without his knowledge—jewelry, ceramics.

When he eventually discovered evidence of those, he

hadn't gotten as angry, but it was also clear he didn't think she took any of it seriously. Besides, the things she had made, they were useful. He was all for anything useful.

Then her hands became more useful later when she needed to make more money, when go-go dancing, then going topless wasn't enough.

She needed to save up faster for the boob job her friend Elena made clear was necessary; according to Elena, her flat, 32A chest was why she only made around three hundred a night. Elena said she could go up to a thousand with bigger boobs—that men gladly pay lots more for those.

Melanie wasn't sure at first because men seemed to like her as she was. They liked her pale and skinny, and even liked her hair. It made them smile and say things like: "You are so adorable, honey—what are you, thirteen? Your mommy let you cut your hair like that?"

She never mentioned she didn't have a mommy.

Melanie knew they liked everything about her because she was so young and looked it. Still, she figured Elena was right, having been in the business longer, and Melanie agreed to start hand jobs to make more money faster for the boobs she would need as she got older.

Her father wasn't happy when he discovered her compromise—he had no appreciation for her way of making money through becoming living art, bought over and over again. He had turned into a beast and she ran away from his anger only to show up at his door in tears a few weeks later because her work family now wanted her to use more than her hands on clients. On top of that, if she had overheard correctly, they had very bad things planned for her, far beyond convincing her to sleep with repulsive men.

When her father calmed down, her cheek still burning from his palm, he agreed to let her back in his house on one condition. *Purgatory*, he had called the camp, and she had only a vague impression of what he meant. Still, she gladly agreed—the camp was nothing compared to what awaited her at *Val's Valley*, and how dirty and smelly the place was, became much clearer once she settled in her old room again.

Melanie had begun feeling alone at her job. The girls were ultra-competitive, and not shy about their jealousy—especially lately, with men going wild over the addition of gloves to her outfits. One girl even threatened to cut her face. Another teased her about her breasts all the time, but Melanie knew she was just insecure because she was so much older—about thirty or so with eye wrinkles—and had to wear lots of makeup to cover it up. Melanie thought it laughable how this woman pretended to be much younger. *Twenty-four*, she told everyone. Ha! What a joke. Everyone knew she was lying—she looked even older than her real age. She did have really good boobs though, and had been working in the place a long time. She knew pole tricks and had regulars seeking her out, bringing her gifts.

After working at "The Valley" for a bit, Melanie began to realize the girls she had considered friends slipped snide remarks to and about her here and there, that she had no real friends.

The last straw was overhearing a group of girls joke about setting her up for a Basketball team train. "That'll break her," she heard one say, as if she needed more breaking. Later, when she confronted one of the girls about it, the girl insisted the group had just been playing around, that they always joked like that.

Melanie knew she had to leave, but when she told her mentor about her plans, the woman got really angry and said she couldn't.

Melanie decided to sneak out instead, so she pretended to change her mind, to the delight of her mentor, who soon arranged her first motel 'date.'

The man was fat and bald and completely disgusting, but Melanie stomached his arm around her shoulders and a slap on the butt on the way to his room. Once they got there, and he pushed her down in front of him for the first part of his service, she bit his balls so hard that she had time to get up and run out of the room. She kept running, then hid until she was sure he wouldn't find her. Then she found her way back to her dad's.

Now she had only three weeks until she was safely

home again with her father, where she could get back to her pottery, and wouldn't have to take off her clothes, or think about her small tits. Where she wouldn't feel so vulnerable and unprotected.

She thought enduring this wilderness program would be a breeze as long as she had her trusty companions with her, but she had gone and dropped one in this damned forest.

She flicked on the light again and checked her clothes. Maybe it had gotten caught in a fold...

She searched the ground around her again and again.

Finally, she wept quietly in defeat.

She had planned so carefully, needed it so badly! And now it was gone.

If only it wasn't so damned dark!

She pulled out another of her treasured smuggled objects and ran its edge over an untouched part of her thigh. She leaned her head back against the tree, enjoying the brief pain, the wetness of new blood drops.

She also had plans for the slight bit of paper it came wrapped in, decorated in her own blotter art.

Then she snapped her head forward at another sound.

As she jerked, the razor found itself deeper in her skin, making her flinch more than usual.

What could it be? What kind of animal had the kind of snorting breath...?

Then she heard a sort of chomping, clacking sound.

She also suddenly realized how deep a wound she had made in her thigh and tried not to panic, but she shot straight up, trying to think how she could stem this flow, how she would be able to hide it besides pretending she embarrassingly got caught in the wilderness at the wrong time of the month. That awful large boy would surely not let her hear the end of it.

The thought faded as the odd, snorting breath became louder, and seemed to circle her. She had the distinct impression she was being stalked, and at any moment, the source of the strange sounds would come at her.

She now regretted running so far away from the camp —although she had only meant to hide away for a moment.

"Is it you, Jake?" she asked the dark hopefully, flickering her pathetic light. For now, nothing—not even the thought of Bluto—frightened her more than not knowing what the sound was or where it was coming from.

She didn't have to wait long as galloping footsteps crashed through the bush, and a loud chomping and grunting topped off by a horrible squeal preceded a creature revealing itself to her.

A shrill, piercing, animalistic scream left her own body.

———

Jake was not completely surprised by Melanie's actions—he had dealt with highly emotional kids before, even someone running off, then eventually returning. In the end, they always came back with their tail between their legs, realizing it was better to be with a group of strangers—some of whom they perhaps didn't like off the bat—than alone in a wilderness.

Kids who acted out this way realized they didn't know the first thing about the area, and they were young enough that they still had large imaginations. They probably thought any number of beasties could be out there waiting to get them.

Jake liked letting them think that—it made them rely on him despite any tendency they had to rebel.

It was why he took them off the beaten path—to enforce that feeling—but it raised the stakes for him too.

When Jake heard Melanie scream, he got an awful feeling in his stomach—a strong impression that Melanie would not have a chance.

The scream helped him locate her, and after a few minutes of following the sound, he came upon the area where he felt she was nearby.

The forgotten walkie-talkie clipped to him buzzed to life, and he quickly briefed a curious Eric on his progress while his flashlight lit the way to Melanie's broken body.

She bled from several puncture wounds, the crimson, scattered blood contrasting stunningly with the emerald canvas of moss carpeting the forest floor like a gorgeously macabre painting.

She appeared to have been gored, then tossed against the tree, but he saw no claw marks or other signs of a bear.

Her body was unnaturally propped up on wide roots, her limbs yielding around the folds.

The attack had splashed her face with blood, leaving only her frozen blue eyes unstained.

The first thing Jake felt as her death sunk in was a deep, seasoned melancholy. He silently mourned the young girl who clearly didn't have a chance against whatever had decided to attack her alone in the dark, unpredictable forest.

Then he felt anger: what the hell possessed her to run off like that, so far away from safety in these conditions? They were both now a good half-mile from the campsite.

The next thing Jake felt was worry—how could something like this happen on his watch? Since the inception of WISH, he had never experienced such a tragedy; everyone always came back alive, and furthermore, better human beings.

The next thing Jake wondered was what on earth he would tell the girl's parents. And then he remembered—it was just her dad. But breaking the news to just one parent wouldn't necessarily be easier; what could he say to that obviously hardworking, determined man he had met? How could he tell him that the daughter he so believed he could help with tough love was now ripped open, having found herself on the wrong end of...what the hell was that, anyway?

Jake knew he was dealing with something very serious, and decided to give Eric a heads up about the danger so the group could be on guard.

As he re-clipped the walkie-talkie, Jake's next thought was how and when they would be able to transport the body. He knew it was best not to touch it at all—he couldn't exactly administer first aid; the girl was beyond help. He would have to make a call, breaking the isolation he had so carefully prepared for and constructed, to bring in real authorities.

The last thing Jake thought about was how vulnerable he himself was at that moment, until he heard movement through the forest—the unmistakable sound of a charging animal heading his way.

Whatever had attacked Melanie was coming back.

Jake braced himself, then cursed when he realized he didn't have his gun, remembering the backpack he had left behind in his dash for the girl. But he always kept his KA-BAR on him, so he drew it, despite thinking the Marine Corps knife might not be a match for what had torn up Melanie.

He figured it was probably best to run, but didn't dare reduce himself to it; instead, he stood his ground, ready to take on whatever was about to burst through.

But instead of a bear, or Freddy Krueger, or even a wild tiger escaped from a zoo, out emerged a terrified-looking man who smashed into him, apparently in his own mad dash to escape something—Jake still wasn't sure what. They collided and crashed to the ground, his knife flying from his hand.

Jake then realized he had a pain in his lower abdomen as he lay on his back.

The man began pulling himself off of him, and Jake felt every bit of the withdrawal of an impressive-looking knife from his stomach, glistening with blood.

Then he looked down at himself and saw the blood leaking from him, staining his yellow shirt.

When he looked up again, the man's already terrified face looked even more frightened, but more than that, it looked apologetic as he seemed to study one of his outstretched arms. Jake tried to think of what could be fascinating him so. Was it the Recon Jack tattooed on the inside of his bicep? Jake had been so proud of how the various elements had come together, as if he had done the artwork himself; the skull, knife, wing, paddle and diver blending into one seamless design.

"Oh my god, I didn't mean to..."

The man's eyes almost looked comical to him—glassy, wide and almost downturned as a darkness began climbing over his vision.

He started feeling lightheaded, and the air seemed to take on an almost dreamlike appearance.

The last thing Jake saw before losing consciousness was the man's face collapsing further into sorrow and worry, his fingers touching his face gently.

Then the last thing he heard was:

"I'm so sorry, brother—it was after me, just killed my friend, and I thought you were...I was just—"

FIVE

HOGS ON ICE

W hen Melanie screamed, the kids all shut up immediately, sharply aware at last of dangers beyond the fortress of their semicircle of tents.

Eric watched the fight or flight instinct activate in each of them—ears tuned to the night, eyes darting, bodies confused as to what to do next.

There was no doubt who the feminine shriek had come from, since neither Melanie nor Jake had returned.

Suddenly, one of the boys began to rise, as if to investigate.

"Don't even think about it," Eric said, freezing him in place. "I can't have you kids running off into trouble like that."

Then Eric realized the boy was the youngest of the lot, and also that he was the only one who had instinctively responded to the obvious cry for help.

Eric tried to reach Jake on his walky-talky. "Jake, you there? Jake?"

Jake's voice sounded odd, muffled—but also like he was running when it finally came.

"I'm here," he said.

"Find the girl?"

"Not yet, but you bet I'm...oh my god."

Eric's blood froze.

He realized the kids had heard the whole exchange and their eyes were probably on him, looking for a cue about how to respond—perhaps seconds away from panicking.

He was now temporarily in charge, he remembered, so he consciously made himself look relaxed, releasing the tension in his shoulders, counting to three while taking a deep breath, letting his legs relax slowly until they came to rest slightly open once again. He released the tightened muscles in his forehead, separating his eyebrows.

He knew he had to control his body language, that these kids probably picked up on every nuance. The things he heard they had done—they probably had more "street smarts" than the average kid their age.

"Eric," Jake said through the speaker, "just stay there with the kids. And listen to me—you better arm yourself. Start getting ready to get those kids the hell out of here until we figure out what's going on."

Arm myself? Eric thought. *Arm myself with what?*

And before considering any of the weapons he knew Jake had left behind in his backpack, Eric closed his eyes and turned to the best weapon he had: he offered up a prayer, his biggest defense right now, as ever.

When he silently said amen, Eric knew he could make an army of these kids if he needed to.

His mind went back to Jake and Melanie.

What had Jake found out there? He had never heard Jake use such a tone—wonder and terror churned into a whisper. After running these camps for so long, what could have struck him with such awe?

Eric didn't realize he had kept his eyes closed until they opened and immediately found the concerned dark eyes of the young, black boy who had almost followed Jake into the forest at Melanie's scream looking back at him. He had such a young, sweet face—the only indicator of his age.

"Don't worry, son, everything's going to be all right," Eric said, smiling at him, fully believing his own words.

The boy tentatively smiled back as though not sure, but Eric could tell he wanted to believe him.

He would show the young one he was right, that everything would be okay because God would never put more on him than he could bear. This was only a test.

THE SILENCE WAS DEAFENING, each second an hour.

Eric tried not to panic or let his nerves show, but Jake should have been back by now—or at least given some kind of update. Eric hadn't heard anything else from him, despite calling to him over the walkie-talkie over and over again, and he couldn't help but think the worst.

He became aware of the pairs of young eyes watching him again, the kids seemingly too terrified to move even a facial muscle.

Had it been five minutes since their last exchange, or twenty?

Eric settled on the largest of the children.

"You, there—what's your name again?"

The large boy looked at him, answering a few seconds after his face had gathered into a scowl.

"Bluto," he said.

"Yes, that's right—Christopher."

Eric figured two could play the game. He preferred to use the boy's given, Christian name anyway.

"Son, I'm going to head on out there and see what's going on, and I'm gonna leave you in charge since you're the oldest and likely, the most mature." He addressed the group. "Everybody just stay calm and stay put till we get back, Jake and me...and Melanie. Shouldn't be too long."

Then Eric looked over at the bag Jake left behind.

He had to do it—it would be stupid not to.

Eric dug into the bag for Jake's weapon.

His dad had taken him on a shooting range when he was a teen—he could still hit something if he needed to—he hoped. Still, his hands shook as he withdrew the gun from the bag.

He didn't want to have to use it, but it made no sense to traipse into the night forest unarmed after hearing a scream like they had heard. Man or animal—something was out there causing trouble, and with Jake having followed it, Eric needed something to protect himself, and perhaps Jake. Ultimately, it would help protect these defenseless children, and he needed to do what was right for the greater good.

———

EVERYONE STARED at the beckoning backpack, stealing glances at each other. There was no doubt they were all thinking the same thing—raid the bag.

Jake's backpack was one hell of a bag compared to theirs—babies in comparison. Joe figured there had to be tons of valuables in it—perhaps a satellite phone they could use, another gun, a flame-thrower—who knew? All they knew was that they were in a wilderness, and something had gone very wrong. Melanie might not come back, Jake hadn't come back, and Eric might not make it back; they would be stupid not to raid it. Even if Eric did return, they were undeniably in danger—something was out there, and they were sitting ducks without weapons or anything that could protect them from it.

Joe's heart was still beating rapidly from witnessing Eric pull a bad-ass looking gun from the bag. He hoped there were more weapons inside.

He made a move just as everyone else did, and they all made a run for the backpack at the same time.

Narine happily grabbed a set of keys—presumably an extra set to the van that brought them all here.

Bug spray. Mace. A first aid kit. A journal. Bullets.

Items flew across Joe's vision, barely registering as he thought about the other possible weapon or two—what they needed most of all.

And then, bingo—the mother of all knives.

Joe was the first to grab it, but unlike the bug spray or the journal, this item did not escape other eyes.

Bluto stared at him, and it was clear it didn't matter that Joe had gotten to it first. Bluto easily snatched the blade from him then shoved him to the ground. Bluto was undoubtedly bigger and stronger, but Joe didn't want to back down. It wasn't a matter of the item itself now, but the principle: Bluto shouldn't be allowed to think he could just shove people around like that.

But Joe decided to leave the giant alone with his prize —maybe he could find something else of value instead of wasting time fighting over what he had already lost.

THIS WAS TRULY A TEST.

Of what, and on what—Eric didn't know, but God was testing him severely.

His stomach held up after finding the two bodies near each other—the teenaged girl almost ripped to pieces, Jake bleeding out from a single gash.

Eric thought maybe if he had gotten on the move faster, he would have been able to save Jake since he had only one wound, whereas the girl had...

Bile began rising in his throat again.

Phone! Yes, of course he had a satellite phone—needed to call for help. But that would mean being distracted, maybe putting the gun down in an area where some murderous creature had just been while he dug through his bag. Putting himself at risk all alone here, perhaps too far away from the campsite for anyone to be able to reach him on time.

He would have to wait until he returned to the camp grounds, where he figured he should probably start heading back right now, but the gory scene entranced him, appearing surreal almost—save for the heavy stench of death.

Eric had been so excited to join Jake on this trip after having finally convinced him he could be an asset.

He met Jake at church funnily enough, considering

Jake's opposition to him making this camp appear like a Christian wilderness retreat in any way.

Jake had started showing up on Sundays, looking reluctant each time, and they ended up in small-talk at one of the church's monthly luncheons.

Eric was impressed when he found out what Jake did: a wilderness retreat for teens? What a great idea! And something they could probably bring to the church in some form.

Jake declined to run it himself—the way he ran his camp was one thing; taking out a bunch of church kids was altogether different, he had said.

Eric began flirting with the idea of running a similar program for the church kids himself. As church event coordinator, in charge of programs like the luncheons, maybe he could add being a camp leader to his list of duties. It would be another wonderful way to serve his master, while allowing time to admire His creations in the wild.

Eric asked Jake's permission to accompany him on a trip so he could see what it was like and get a better idea of what he would be getting into.

When Jake eventually agreed, he explained his philosophy, made him go through first aid and CPR training amongst others, talked to him about previous retreats and kids, what to expect.

Luckily, Eric had been a Boy Scout and remembered a

few basics regarding reading compasses and such; in fact, he still had a compass his dad had given him with a cross on it. He had brought it along for this, his first trip.

He did, however, need a few refresher courses—Jake didn't take the role of his assistant lightly since he needed someone competent, capable, and useful at his side.

Jake talked about previous guides, and what they had brought to the table, and they had all been processed in a similar manner.

Jake had even run a background check on him, despite knowing he was a churchgoing man who wanted nothing more than to find a way to help kids, expand their minds and hearts. Save their souls.

By the end of it all, Eric felt prepared for the trip in every way but one—mentally.

He was still a little apprehensive about the grade of kids—from what Jake had told him, these kids were not at all your regular hormonal kids acting out.

Eric had a teenaged niece and his brother talked about the grief she caused him—having to ground her for sneaking out to parties and eighteen-plus clubs and things like that. And she apparently had a much older boyfriend.

All of that sounded like headache enough.

But the WISH kids were on a whole other level, and Eric was glad Jake was so strong and confident a leader, so rooted in his philosophy even if it meant being dismissive about Eric's own ideas about how to reach the kids.

Eric marveled at how Jake seemed unintimidated by the teenagers, and figured it might take more than one trip for that kind of confidence to rub off on him.

But now, by some horrible twist of fate, Eric's first trip turned out to be Jake's last.

Poor guy. After four solid years to come face to face with...what?

Eric examined the wounds on the girl again, and this time he couldn't help it—he threw up.

It wasn't the same thing—whatever had killed the girl —maybe a bear, or some type of wild cat—hadn't killed Jake; Jake looked like he had been stabbed.

He noticed something stuck to the girl's hand—a brightly colored piece of paper—and he bent to examine it further. He removed the tiny piece of artwork, puzzling over it for a moment. He figured it might be important, something the girl's family might want—a sort of final keepsake. He decided to hold on to it.

His eyes quickly scanned the forest for any movement. Then he finally admitted to himself that there was indeed one thing missing from his preparation. He had gone through light medical training and wilderness basics. He knew how to make a fire, follow a compass, and locate the nearest source of water. But as he fiddled with Jake's gun and realized the safety was on, he also realized he didn't really know how to fire this particular weapon. Didn't even know if it was loaded.

Being around the grisly sights and smells didn't help his mental processes, but his body responded, and he began feeling woozy, and nauseous.

The rest of his sandwich, fruit, and cookie from earlier that day came up easily.

Eric knew he had to get back to the kids, but before venturing on to the campsite in front of all those young, frightened, enquiring eyes, he had to talk to His Father once again; he needed guidance now more than ever.

SIX

THE LEGEND OF HOGZILLA

When the sound of running footsteps intruded upon the night, Joe immediately thought it was Eric—perhaps Jake—running back to them, and they all looked eagerly in its direction, hiding away their plundered goods. The footsteps also put an end to Joe's thoughts about maybe going after Bluto while he was distracted.

But the face that emerged from the forest was an unfamiliar one, the body soiled with bits of dirt and reddish mud. The man looked so scared—almost like a trapped animal—that Joe felt no threat at his approach, despite the elongated shiny object in his left hand he quickly hid behind him. He was a man they could probably outrun if they needed to—he looked exhausted from running as he bent over and put his hands on his knees, taking deep breaths, clearly not threatened by them either; in fact, he appeared relieved to see them.

Once he had breathed deeply for a while, he walked closer to them, examining them.

Joe realized their shirts had grabbed his attention, and for a moment it seemed the man was reliving something. Joe realized something else, and he suspected he wasn't alone either: the red mud on him—it looked like blood.

"Your leader," was all the man said, and they remained silent, watching him. Waiting. The man tilted his head back a bit as his eyes closed briefly. "It was your leader..."

"Okay, what are you talking about, lame-o, and what about our leader?" said Narine, looking as if she was preparing to say something even nastier to the stranger. She was staring at one of his legs.

Then Joe, too, noticed something amiss—something unnatural about one of his lower limbs.

The man headed to the log where Jake and Eric had sat previously—an obvious open seat, and perfect placement in front of them, still catching his breath, it seemed.

"I know it's still out there," the stranger began, making Joe nervous. "I heard the squeal and the chomping. You guys better go—get up out of here before it gets you."

They all sat in silence, staring, not making a single move.

Despite his clean shave and short hair, the man looked

almost feral, his eyes wild. What had he seen? What disturbed and terrified him so?

"Get on with it," Bluto said, pulling out Jake's knife and clearly making sure the man saw it. "Who the fuck are you and why should we listen?"

The man fixed his eyes on him. "I'm Nathan Colt, and we have a giant, feral hog stalking us right now."

Joe heard someone giggle, but couldn't tell who it was.

"Look, we used to have a boar problem around here years ago, but then it was open season, and hunters ended up killing 'em so fast, that a few guys started breeding up more just for trophies—a mix and match of different breeds to get the biggest ones. People would report seeing a giant one in particular here or there over the years, but it was supposed to be like a Bigfoot thing; nobody took it seriously. But I'm telling you—this thing is real, and it is a monster."

"Like Hogzilla!" Ralph said, sounding inexplicably excited.

Joe didn't think all the man was saying necessarily true, but figured they better listen without interrupting. He respected the strange man—not only because he was the only adult around at the moment and seemed like he had an idea of what was going on, but because the shiny object he had glimpsed left an impression.

"Unfortunately for us, the bigger the hog, the smarter it is, and they can easily smell human scent from a mile away. Plus, they can outrun the fastest human. That girl didn't have a chance; she was with you guys, I believe—had on that same yellow shirt, like your leader."

"Yeah, but what about our leader? We've got two of them—although I'd hardly count one of them," Narine said.

Joe felt a general reluctance in the air, a distrust. The man hadn't convinced any of the others of anything it seemed, besides maybe being crazy.

The man looked up then, staring at the sky for a few moments.

Joe looked up to see what he was looking at and saw nothing but stars.

Then the man looked back down and seemed to notice the shiny knife at his side for the first time. He wiped the knife off on his pants, then drew a second blade from a holster at his hips—one that looked like the one Jake had—and stared at it.

"He's dead, I'm afraid," he said to the group. "It wasn't from the pig, though—the pig got the girl—I could tell by her wounds. Poor little thing never had a chance—she was gutted like a fish by those tusks. But unfortunately for your leader, he met my knife."

A sharp intake of breath all around followed, as the man's eyes went back to the first blade.

The stranger seemed deeply affected by the

confession, sinking further into the suit of filth that coated him.

"It was an accident," he emphasized as his eyes came back to them. "That damned animal took out a friend of mine a while ago, and I've been running from it since. Didn't know you guys would be around here—didn't think anything but getting away, out of this forest. With this knife in my hand, running through the trees, I collided with him, and he met with the wrong end of this." He held up the blade in his right hand. "He knew I didn't mean it, and I tried to fix him—I worked on him right away, tried to stem the flow of blood but..." He shook his head.

Then he touched the knife's tip, silent for a few moments.

Joe sensed a change among the group, an openness that hadn't been there before—like they were starting to believe the man. Even Bluto didn't look so brave now.

Joe couldn't think of anything to say, and it seemed like no one else could either. All Joe knew was that the guy who had all the answers was gone—probably the only one who could get them out of the forest safely. And now Eric, the only other person they had a shot with, might not return.

"Listen, if you guys have any connection at all with the outside world, I suggest you call for help. I'm not here to entertain you—just letting you know what's out there.

Now, get the hell out of here. Again, sorry about your leader and all."

And with that, he stood to leave.

"But which way do we go?" Luz asked with what looked like panic in her eyes.

The man turned back toward them, then pointed at the sky with the knife.

"You see that star right there? That's the direction y'all want to head."

"Maybe we should wait till Eric gets back," Luz said.

"He might not come back," Narine replied.

"Who's Eric?" the man asked suddenly.

"That other leader I mentioned," Narine said impatiently. "He went off to find Jake and hasn't come back yet, but we also haven't heard anything weird since he left, so he might still be alive."

"Well, again, I suggest you kids start moving. If he's still alive, he'll find you. No use waiting to see if it's him or that hog crashing through the bushes at you."

And then, inexplicably reenergized, he headed in the opposite direction he told them to go.

"Thought you said you were trying to get out of here?" Narine said, raising her voice after the departing figure.

"I sure am," he said without turning around. "But not without bringing that pig's head back with me. I made it through Recon selection and two tours of Iraq—I'm not getting scared off by some feral pig. He killed my friend, and I'm not lettin' that go easy."

Joe wanted to ask him how he expected to take the monster down if it was as big as he thought it was. The man's weapons—while impressive—couldn't take the beast down at a safe distance. And then there was that leg...

"Pigs can't climb trees," the man said as if reading his thoughts. "I'll wait it out, wait till it gets light. Maybe you guys should too—you have a better chance in the daytime. No sleep tonight," he said. Then he trotted off.

They all exchanged looks, and Joe figured everyone else was as confused about the man as he was. But one thing was clear: they were on their own.

They started packing up their tents—no way would they be sitting ducks at night.

"I wonder if we should just leave these here," Luz said, surveying the tents.

"I think we should definitely take them—who knows if we'll make it out of here by tomorrow?" Ralph said.

"Yeah, but it took us, what, six hours to hike here? Why should it take more than twenty-four hours to get back to where the van dropped us off? I don't see any reason we should weigh ourselves down with more than we need. We have water, and if we run out, we should run into it somewhere along the way. We have a couple of snacks..."

"Yeah, and Ralph here knows how to make fires, right, Ralph?" Bluto said snidely.

"I mean, who would actually sleep while we're stuck in this forest with some horrible creature on the loose?" Luz continued.

"Well, we should take at least *one* nap, don't you think? Like have two people on night watch while everyone takes turns if it really comes to that?" Narine said.

"Brilliant, Narine. Get that beauty sleep in while you can with some hybrid beast running around," Ralph said quietly.

Before Narine could respond, Luz said: "Between the six of us, we can figure out how to get out of here by daylight. Now, who here is good with direction?"

Narine giggled. "The irony," she said as explanation.

"I am," David replied, surprising Joe since he had forgotten all about him once he had gone off to pee, missing the stranger's speech.

"Don't worry—I heard the important parts from the bushes," David said, looking into each surprised face.

"Good, so we'll start with what that weirdo said..."

"You really want to trust that guy?" asked Narine.

"Do we really have any other choice right now? Anyone else know exactly which way to go to get the fuck back?" Bluto replied.

Silence.

"It's really hard to tell when it's dark like this," Ralph piped up. "If it was daytime..."

"Yeah, but it's not, so...anyone else got anything useless to say?"

"I just think..." Luz began, "...well, what if that guy was mistaken and we end up going the wrong way for a couple of hours?"

"Okay, who else thinks it's better to keep moving—even if in the wrong direction—rather than stay here and wait to be killed?" Narine asked. "I mean, it looks like it's the right direction—away from that animal anyway. Melanie's scream came from that way." She pointed opposite of where the man had directed them. "Plus, we just need to find some trees where we can maybe wait the darkness out, or at the very least, climb to safety if we need to."

No one objected.

As they continued gathering their things, Luz spoke up once more.

"But what about Eric? Shouldn't we wait for him? As far as we know, he's not dead yet."

Then, as if on cue, a masculine voice emitted a horrible scream.

The sound rippled through the air, standing Joe's hair on end.

Even Narine's composure briefly slipped as she whispered: "Oh my god."

Joe wasn't sure if it was the strange man or Eric, but it was all he needed to go along with Narine's plan.

"It sounded close—could've been either," Ralph said.

"I think it came from that weird man," Luz replied.

"Was probably Eric—he looks like he'd scream like that," Narine said, recovering.

"Who gives a fuck which one it was?" Bluto asked. "All we know is one more person is probably toast. I don't care if it's a bear that did it, some fuckin' nutcase, or a crazy, fat pig—let's get the hell out of here."

With no room for disagreement and armed with their flashlights and anything else they thought useful for defense, they began their trek.

SEVEN

IN A PIG'S EYE

The howl got Eric's attention—who had been attacked this time?

It had to be one of the kids or some other unfortunate soul who had decided to hike tonight. Most likely the latter —the howl hadn't come from the direction of the campsite, nor did it sound like one of the young boys; the holler was an adult male's.

Eric figured when he got back to the camp, he would gather up the kids to start heading back right away—he knew how to get them out of there fast.

Jake had taken him on a dry run through the general areas they would hit in the forest, and went through a more extensive explanation on a map. He had pointed out key spots that gave an idea of location in relation to the trail beginning.

Eric took another deep breath.

He could do this—he could get the rest of the kids back to safety.

Not only that, he could show them the way to redemption.

Jake had told him to "go light on the Jesus talk" because not everyone would be receptive to his approach; not everyone would have grown up in a household that accepted his faith as any sort of truth. Jake said that pushing his Christianity and the Bible hard could be a grave mistake, and might have the opposite effect of what they were going for. That the kids might rebel, close themselves up. That they were all there because they needed something more concrete than biblical verses—not that he didn't believe, he was sure to insist.

Still, Eric had pressed: the kids needed to know, whether they had family members on their side or not, that God loves them; it could only help. But Jake had shot him down.

And now it appeared to be God's will for him to take over.

He would get the chance to hand the kids the list he had made for them in case Jake changed his mind and let him get his way a little.

He called it the ABC's of redemption:

A - All have sinned and come short of the glory of God.
B - Believe on the Lord Jesus Christ and thou shalt be saved.

C - Children obey your parents in the Lord for this is right.
D - Depart from evil, and do good.
E - Even a child is known by his doings...

And on and on all the way to Z.

How could Jake not see how relevant it was?

———

"So what do you guys think about that pig story?" Narine asked. "Think there's really some giant hog tracking people down just to kill them?"

"I think he watches too much TV or something," David said.

"I'm pretty sure he was exaggerating about it targeting people specifically, but there probably is a wild pig out there somewhere. And who knows? Maybe Melanie tried to snort one of its babies or something," Bluto said.

Narine giggled.

"So it went ahead and attacked her," he continued. "Rightfully so. You don't mess around with someone's babies. Right, Luz? Pig or otherwise."

Luz looked up with an odd expression on her face.

Joe shook his head. There Bluto went again with the fat jokes about Luz. But before he could say anything, Ralph jumped in.

"Maybe Jake found her and she's fine, but they're busy

doing it right now." Ralph grinned, but nobody grinned back.

"I saw a TV show about a giant pig," David said. "Those things look pretty scary when they're in the wild like that—all dark and hairy, and four tusks looking like something from a nightmare—two going up, two going outward. When you usually think of a pig, you think of some harmless animal, maybe something tasty. A pig in a pen, or breakfast on the table. But not these wild ones—they don't even look like you can eat them. I was so surprised to see how a pig could turn into a monster like that; seriously, they're the last thing you'd want to run into in the wild. I'd rather run into a mountain lion."

"But mountain lions can climb trees, right? Wouldn't you rather run into something you can just get away from like that?" Luz said.

"Yeah, but what if the right kind of tree isn't around? How far do you think you'll get with one of those things behind you? You heard the guy—they can outrun the fastest human."

"I just hope that story's not really true," Ralph said. "Or that the pig's already had its fill of man-meat or something, and leaves us alone."

"Honestly, I think it's all a setup," David said, shrugging.

"What do you mean?" asked Narine.

"I mean, there's a chance this is just some sort of prank

or some kind of learning exercise. They probably just hired that blond girl to go along with the whole thing—make it seem like we're in some kind of danger. But I bet this is just to make us let our guards down, start relying on each other for survival, et cetera. You know, all that bull Jake was talking about earlier. I mean, don't you think it's a bit convenient that the two leaders just happened to have been taken out first?"

"I think that's just a matter of them both going off on their own; they put themselves in more danger that way. Even if the forest guy is crazy, there are bears and all kinds of shit out there," Ralph said.

"Well, say we all survive till tomorrow morning with no more attacks. I think you'll all be rethinking my theory."

Joe had to admit to himself that it made some kind of sense—a sort of extreme survival, scared-straight-in-the-forest boot camp.

It could work.

They would have no choice but to get over themselves, learn each other's strengths and weaknesses to improve the chances of the group surviving overall.

"Okay, so David says he's good with direction—what do the rest of you have to bring to the table to get through this?" Narine asked.

Joe went to the nearest tree and with one hand

grabbed a branch and launched himself up into it. "I can help people get up trees," he said.

Ralph flickered a lighter he had acquired. "I can make fire anywhere, with almost anything," he said.

"Don't tell me the rest of y'all are as useless as you look," Bluto said. "I mean, for me it's obvious—I can carry anything. Plus, I'm a natural leader, and the only man here."

"I can cook," Luz said.

"Surprise, surprise," Bluto replied.

"And I can..." Narine began, and Joe was sure she would say something like: "make things pretty" or even just: "look pretty."

Instead she said: "I can drive—for when we get back to the van, if it's there. I'm really good at it."

"You should have just said you can make things pretty," Bluto said, making most of them laugh.

———

Eric knew there was something wrong before he reached the campsite. Everything was a little too quiet—a little too still.

He braced himself.

The kids couldn't have gone to sleep—not with all the commotion.

And then he had a horrible thought—what if they had

all been taken out, silenced by a bear or some other forest beast?

He shook off the thought—surely he would have heard the sounds of an attack going down.

"Kids?" he called out before breaking through the brush.

No response.

When he arrived at the campsite, he saw no physical signs of an attack and that the fire was still going strong, almost beckoning to him.

They don't even know the basic danger of forest fires, he thought, shaking his head, thinking about what could have happened had he not returned to the site.

It fortified him; the kids obviously needed his help.

Before extinguishing the fire, he took a deep breath and looked around the site for clues, noticing a few tents missing.

The teenagers had definitely decided to take off. They probably thought the unknown man in the forest screaming had been him, so he didn't blame them; they had good survival instincts.

They were smart to prepare for possibly spending a night in the wilderness, despite the bear or whatever it was making the deadly attacks.

Eric looked around for signs of the direction they had gone in.

Then he remembered he needed to try to reach

someone, anyone.

He put his bag down and took out his satellite phone.

His heart sank when he realized he couldn't dial or anything, that the battery had likely died and he had not only forgotten to charge it, but left behind his spare.

Still, he wasn't concerned—once he found the kids, they would make it back out of the wilderness within a day.

It had taken them over six hours to get to the site after that lengthy van ride. They had begun the hike at midday, stopping three times for official half-hour breaks, a few other times for bathroom breaks.

But the kids would probably never make it out in that kind of time themselves, especially at night. He had to find them; he knew how to keep them on the right path, and get them out sooner than later.

Eric made another quick sweep of the site with his eyes.

Jake's open bag sat there, obviously tampered with. How had he missed it before? Of course the kids would have gone through it to help them through their trek.

He wondered what they had taken.

Eric hadn't really registered the contents as he searched for the weapon, and he wasn't there when Jake had packed it, so he didn't know what exactly had been in the backpack. He imagined all the things Jake suggested he bring along himself at the very least.

And, son-of-a-gun—the kids had taken whatever emergency communication device Jake might have had. Eric now had to fully rely on what Jake had taught him, what he himself had learned about the wilderness. He would have to read the signs to figure out where the kids had gone, which was as simple as following the footstep tracks of the group of six, and the broken plants, leaves, and branches they had left behind.

Eric wondered how long ago they had left. In any case, he hadn't left them for very long; they couldn't have gone far. At most, they had a twenty-minute lead on him.

He would find them soon.

————

"AND YOU'RE sure you know where you're going, right?" Narine asked David.

"Isn't this the way that guy pointed us to?" David said irritably.

"Should we really believe him, though?" Ralph asked.

"Yeah—what if he was just plum crazy, or deliberately leading us toward the monster pig? So that while we're getting attacked, he'll have some time to get out of here. You saw him with that leg; he needs all the help he can get for a head start," Bluto said.

"Yeah, I guess you could be right about misdirection—I didn't even think about it like that," David said. "Anyway,

I studied a map of the area before we came here, and I'm pretty sure this happens to be the right way to get out of here."

"Well, we trust you," Narine said.

"It's not like you have any other choice. Anybody else want to be navigator? No? Well, all righty then—guess everyone's gonna shut up about it now," David said firmly.

They all went silent. As the silence stretched on, so did Joe's imagination, and he had to fight against jumping at every sound from the bush.

"So, we didn't really get very far with those introductions," Bluto said suddenly into the quiet. "What are the rest of you guys here for? And Narine, no more of that bullshit. We know you're not here 'cause your mom thinks you're too pretty. Must be something to do with that, though—about your looks and how you use them."

Narine turned away.

"What about you, Ralph?"

"As if you guys don't already know. Last time I lit something on fire, people were in it. No deaths though," he said, waving his hands defensively as if the others would have immediately jumped him. "Human, that is."

Bluto looked interested, but Luz interjected. "What about you, David? Why'd you get sent here?"

David sighed. "Petty theft," he said. "I just do it for fun though, and then I return the item. You know, like my cousin's computer. I hid it for a few days. And then one of my teachers—I hid her stapler, chalks, eraser. Silly stuff like that—no big deal."

"I never have to steal anything," Narine said. "Whether for fun or not. I always get what I want. Guys give me things."

"Oh, so you're a whore," Luz said. "Why am I not surprised?"

"Don't you dare call me a whore, you bloated elephant."

"Shut up," Joe said to Narine.

"Or else what?" Bluto replied, his dark eyes sharpening with a challenge.

Joe sighed. Bluto just wanted to fight and he didn't want to give him the satisfaction of riling him up.

Ten minutes passed before they heard: "There you are!" and knew who it was immediately; the footsteps hadn't seemed threatening and the voice was soft and familiar.

Joe caught Narine's eye roll.

"Kids, wait up! It's me—your leader! By the way, I noticed back there Jake's bag was pretty darned empty—I figured you guys must have divided the goods amongst yourselves. Anyone care to surrender the borrowed items?"

Everyone either looked away or at each other briefly, but they all stayed quiet, silently daring their new 'leader' to try to take the objects back from each of them.

EIGHT

WHEN PIGS FLY

E ric knew they were about seven miles from where the van had dropped them off.

If they could just keep going, they would be safely out of the wilderness and out of the path of whatever creature was on a rampage back there in just a few hours—if they could only keep their energy up after hiking all day. Eric thought he might even be able to impart the gist of his lessons to them within that time.

He hoped they would have questions—he didn't want to carry on a monologue because, without a doubt, they would stop listening, tiring of it all quickly. He needed to find a way to spread the teachings out, make his messages relevant and easier to swallow.

Quoting straight from the Bible probably wouldn't help—he needed to use the kids' language, to find good examples of the biblical morals so the messages wouldn't seem stale.

"So, what did you find out there, Mr. Green? What happened to Mr. Huntsman and Melanie?" Joe asked, finally breaking the silence.

It was not quite how Eric wanted it broken.

He had a flashback of the way Jake looked in death— still somehow looking very strong, but his eyes empty.

Eric knew there was no way he could describe the bodies to the kids—it would be completely irresponsible to talk about the gashes, the slits, the pools of blood, the glassy eyes.

Eric had seen death only once before: his grandaunt had died in the hospital bed as he and a few other family members surrounded her. She had looked as if she had been dried out.

"I...I'm not sure," Eric said, satisfied with the level of honesty in his reply. "We just have to keep moving—we'll figure it all out when we get back."

"Mr. Green, a strange man came to our campsite while you were gone."

Eric stopped in his tracks, heart rate increasing. "What do you mean? Who?"

Joe shrugged. "I don't know, some ex-military dude. He was all scared and talking about a monster in the forests. Nathan Colt."

"Well, that's just ridiculous," Eric began, although he

didn't believe his own words because a monster made some kind of sense—only a monster could have done what he had seen done to Melanie. "What kind of monster was he talking about?"

"A pig," Joe said. "A giant, killer pig. He said it has four huge, razor-sharp tusks. And that someone probably raised it to kill, but no one ever got it. He said wild pigs are really smart, and really dangerous if they feel threatened. And they run faster than people. And..."

"Okay, okay—I get it." Eric wiped his brow. "That all he said? What did he look like?"

This time, Luz jumped in.

"He had a fake leg," she said. "Oh yeah—and he said the pig killed his friend. He ran to get away from the pig himself, and at some point, ran right into Mr. Huntsman. With his knife. And that's how he died. So don't worry, Mr. Green—we know Mr. Huntsman isn't coming back. You don't have to pretend. We know Melanie's a goner too. We just didn't know if he was telling the truth."

Eric had the distinct impression he was still being asked a question.

He let out a breath. "Yes, it's true—I'm afraid Melanie and Jake won't be joining us again," he said.

"What did they look like when you found them?" Bluto asked.

Eric shook his head. "Almost makes sense what that guy said is all I'll say. But I think it's probably a bear or some other logical explanation. I mean, a giant, man-eating hog?" He shook his head. "Anyway, I'm not giving you kids any details—seems like you guys heard enough."

Eric wondered how long the kids would have kept all of that information to themselves. Kids were funny like that—you had to poke them in the right place or press them enough a couple different ways and things came pouring out like a faucet, no matter how quiet or damaged they were.

Then he felt silly withholding what he knew in the first place, his pitiful attempt to protect them.

"Mr. Green, do you think we'll make it out of here alive?" Luz asked. "If that pig decides to come after us..."

"Yeah, but like that guy said: pigs can't climb trees," Ralph replied. "And if we can get to some solid ones fast enough..."

"But what if we can't?"

"I already told you, there's no monster pig—it's some mountain lion or something, in which case, trees won't help. But whatever's out there, my dear children, pray. Trust God whenever you're afraid, and by looking to Him, you will be saved."

Eric wasn't sure if it was his imagination, but something told him the kids were more receptive, that they had relaxed with his presence. That this was the perfect time for his words.

ERIC DOUBLE-CHECKED HIS COMPASS. They'd had to adjust their path a bit, but now they were definitely on the right track out of the wilderness, and had been going for an hour straight.

"Say, none of you kids happened to come across a GPS device Jake left behind, did you? With emergency calling capability?"

As expected, none of the kids confessed.

"How long is it gonna take to get out of here?" Ralph asked.

"It's hard to say from where we started, but I can't imagine more than a day. And, if we don't take a break, sooner than later."

"Oh my god, I don't think I can make it without a break," Luz said.

"There's a shocker. Fat and lazy," Bluto replied.

"You fat tub of shit—the fuck are you talking about?" Joe said, and as Bluto turned to him, Eric cried:

"Kids! This ain't gonna help—fighting like this. All you're doing is exhausting your energy with all that aggression and negativity. And you, there," he said to Luz, "you shouldn't call the name of the Lord in vain—it's one of the commandments, and I know you know them, being a church girl yourself."

"Oh, I'm no church girl, Mr. Green."

"Don't be ashamed, girl—repeat after me: 'Thou...'" He stopped to cough, trying to bring up the bug that had suddenly flown in his mouth and seemed to lodge in his throat. He cleared his throat and tried again. "Thou shalt not take the name of the Lord thy God in vain.'"

He paused, waiting for her repetition which she gave reluctantly, repeating clumsily while Bluto laughed.

"And you there, boy, repeat after me," Eric said to Bluto. "This one's from that list I handed you—those ABCs of Bible verses I gave you guys to memorize..." He stopped, unable to ignore Bluto having already started repeating after him.

"Okay, now stop it, Christopher. This one's for you: 'K —Keep thy tongue from evil.' Psalm 34:13. Go on now."

And Bluto repeated every single word, including the phrase 'go on now.'

Eric ignored him. "Now listen, I don't want y'all to be scared—ain't nothin' but God's work out there, and He's with you at all times. Just remember He's looking after you, and that's all that matters. Don't be afraid to pray if you're feeling scared or unsure. And don't let your friends here discourage you; in fact, all of you repeat after me: 'Believe on the Lord Jesus Christ and thou shalt be saved.'"

Luz and Joe started to repeat, but seemed to realize they were the only ones and joined the others in silence.

"Okay, fine. But even if you have to pull me aside to

help you, or do it when you go for a bathroom break or something because you're too self-conscious, just do it."

They plodded on.

Half an hour later, Luz was clearly having difficulty again.

"Mr. Green, I can't..." she began, sweating despite the cool night air, cheeks flushed.

"Here we go again," Bluto said. "We could just leave you behind."

"Fuck you—we've literally been hiking all day with these heavy-ass bags going almost nonstop since morning. Look, I'm tired; I can't go any further. I mean, how long did we get to sit at the campsite before things started going down?"

"Well, that's just too damned bad. Hopefully, you can keep the pig at bay while we get away. Maybe it'll try to mate with you."

"Bluto..." Joe began.

"Shut up, super Negro—how many times do I have to floor you for you to realize not to mess with me?"

"Hey, don't act like I'm the only one who's tired, asshole, look at Narine—she looks like she wants to drop any minute too. But oh no, you won't say anything bad about her because you probably think you're gonna hit that little skank," Luz said.

Eric ignored all the profanity and glanced at Narine, who had looked up at them. It was clear she, too, had very little left in her—the glam girl he had met now almost looked like she had spent a day living on the streets.

He looked closely at the other kids.

For all his huffing and puffing, Bluto also looked like he was fighting hard against fatigue and slowly losing. Ralph's face was red and he was walking a bit like he had hurt his foot.

The only kids who still seemed like they had at least another hour or two in them were Joe and David.

"Is there some way we can protect ourselves if we were to stop and make camp for the night?" Joe asked, looking at Luz.

"I can make it so we're in a protective circle of fire," Ralph said, managing a small grin. "That'll keep the pig out."

"And us in and fried once it crawls in on us. God, what a stupid thing to say," Narine said softly, her voice almost like it had come from far away.

"That was obviously a joke, you cunt," Ralph said, shocking Eric—Ralph didn't look like the kind of kid who would emit such foul language. The boy was small for his age, wore glasses, and generally did not look tough. Certainly not enough to back up his words.

"Kids, easy! Ralph, don't you ever let me hear you use that word again—would you use it on your mother? Would you care if someone else used it on her? Now you go ahead and file that word away in your mental circular cabinet and don't even think about using it against a woman again. Go on and repeat what I told Christopher earlier: 'Keep thy tongue from evil.'"

Ralph mumbled his repeat.

Eric noticed Ralph's eyes go to his waist before repeating, and suddenly realized why his words carried any sort of weight at all out here, why he had a bit of power over them and they heeded his requests to repeat anything. Why they stopped attacking each other when he said the word: he still had Jake's gun handy.

Eric almost laughed then. If they only knew how unlikely he was to ever shoot anything. Although, should push come to shove and that monster pig came at them, he hoped he had it in him to shoot that single creature to protect these six, if he could figure the weapon out.

He suddenly felt empowered. "I'll stay up," he said. "We can make camp and I'll let you rest for maybe an hour before we get started again. I'll keep an eye on things out here."

"Can you even use that thing?" Bluto asked, indicating the weapon at his waist.

"My dad taught me to shoot some years ago—probably when I was about your age. I didn't know why, and couldn't imagine ever having to use the skill then, but now I'm glad he did." He saw no use in mentioning he had learned with a completely different kind of gun.

"Well, I used to be a Boy Scout," David suddenly said. "And it's always good to be prepared."

Eric scouted out a clearing on his map, led the group there, and they set up camp.

———

THE FIRE LICKED THE NIGHT.

Tents were up since the kids said they helped them feel a bit more secure than just a sleeping bag.

When Eric told the kids they had an hour to rest, he saw the disappointed looks on both the girls' faces. Time was too precious, however, and although most probably wished for more resting time, he knew they understood the urgency of hiking out of the wilderness as fast as possible.

Still, even he was glad for the reprieve.

David had offered to stay up with him, but Eric insisted the boy rest while he could.

Although David retreated to his tent, Eric noticed his tent lit, and wondered if he needed the flashlight on to help him sleep.

Eric smiled, remembering being like that as a kid—always needing the light on.

Now, in the silent dark, he could regroup and figure out how best to execute his plans. He could double-check the routes, and think about how to adjust this program for his own version. And most of all, he would have time to relax and take in the natural wonders around him, communing with God without speaking a word.

But instead Eric found himself paranoid, listening intently to every sound—every rustle, every groan.

His eyes kept scanning the surrounding forest, looking for—and sometimes seeing—pairs of glowing eyes, his heart leaping, Jake's gun ready.

Every rabbit, every raccoon had him preparing for a showdown.

But as time went on, he found himself relaxing, accepting all the sounds as the innocuous forest sounds they were.

He took in the night sky, appreciating how benevolent it seemed, soft glowing stars welcoming him—like God telling him everything will be all right.

He tried to identify constellations as he sat there—the big dipper over there, Sirius over there. He even thought he saw a shooting star.

He smiled to himself at the quiet beauty above and around him, imagining the little animals that may have been playing or foraging through the forests, although he wasn't sure how many of them were nocturnal: skunks, badgers, possums, raccoons.

He did not imagine a mountain lion or a bear, or even that supposed monster pig—not with the calm that sat around him and the kids that seemed to stretch on for miles.

Eric suddenly got a moment of absolute surety his group would be safe from wild, dangerous animals—at least for the night.

Because of this, he made the decision to let the kids sleep another hour—a gift to them and himself.

He didn't get to enjoy the outdoors much with his office job and church duties keeping him inside most days. And when he went back to his quiet apartment, he found himself just wanting to relax, enjoying the familiarity and comfort of his own home, accountable only to himself and his maker. He could make whatever he wanted to eat for dinner with no time restraints, watch whatever he wanted without outside judgment.

Eric turned his head toward a gentle rustling and noticed David emerging from his tent.

"Can't sleep," the boy said, sitting next to him. "Mind if I watch the fire with you?"

Eric smiled at him. "Don't mind at all."

They sat in silence for a moment. Then David said:

"Mr. Green, do you think it's good that we stopped stoning women like Narine?"

"I beg your pardon?"

"I read it in the Bible. And I know people still do it in other countries. Do you think we should go back to that, or is it like a slippery slope kind of thing since it advocates stoning for quite a lot?"

"David, it's good you're reading the Bible. But that stuff's in the Old Testament. Cultures and times change..."

"Mr. Green, have you ever gotten laid?"

Eric found himself stumbling. "I don't believe that's anyone's business..."

"So which parts do you believe we should stick to?"

Why was this boy flustering him so? It wasn't like he hadn't had to defend himself like this before.

"David, that's quite enough. This isn't the time..."

"But you said if we had any questions..."

"I know, and I'll be happy to talk to you some more, but right now is a perfect time to just give everything a rest till we get going again, don't you think? I promise you I'll talk more about it—we have a few more hours together at least. Now, I have a quick question for you—do you know what this is?" Eric pulled out the tiny, brightly colored piece of paper he had found on Melanie. "I found it on the girl."

"You mean you haven't taken it yet?" David asked, eyes widened.

Eric suddenly felt worried. "What do you mean?"

"You're supposed to put it in your mouth. It helps provide protection against any unclean water we might encounter or bug diseases from bites. See the insect on it? You can get all kinds of illnesses out here if you're not careful. Can't believe Mr. Huntsman didn't tell you."

Eric tried to squelch growing anger at Jake's omission.

Had it been deliberate? Or had he just forgotten? And when did this medicinal administration take place?

"They gave it to us before we met you guys at the van. Anyway, you're brave leaving yourself vulnerable like that."

When David looked away, Eric quickly stuck the paper in his mouth.

As the camp fire began fading a bit, he decided to find more wood to keep it going for the extra time.

He was glad David was still up, and asked him to keep an eye on things until he got back. Then he grabbed his flashlight and made his way carefully into the forest.

As he ventured into the forest, he wished he'd had a large knife with him to cut away at some of the moist bark of the fallen logs to get at the dry, brittle layers.

He saw ahead of him a good candidate for the fire—a massive tree bent and twisted, giving cover to a fallen log sheltering it from the moisture. As he gazed at the massive tree, something odd happened—it smiled at him. It quickly returned to its previous posture, but for a solid moment, the tree contorted itself into a massive smile, distracting him so much, he tripped over an object—a fallen limb, perhaps a sliding stone—then rolled forward. He felt a sharp pain in his side, then the gun in his hand accidentally went off.

Something had pricked him, like the sharp tips of a branch or thorns—stinging nettle maybe, making a deep scrape—but it was a secondary concern to the smiling tree.

Then Eric heard rustling on the forest's surface and knew exactly what had gotten him.

He waved his flashlight around, amazed at the way the beam followed itself, then saw a shimmering, beautiful creature slithering away into the darkness, its brassy-gold scaly body catching the light of the flashlight in such a way that it glowed like a moving golden statue, almost worthy of worship.

Eric shook himself, wondering if his mind was playing tricks on him—a snake god? A smiling tree? What had gotten into him?

The Devil was in the forest.

He had to fight him; this was his battle, his test— something special was happening here.

His mind raced and jumped, but he kept his focus— the kids. He steadied himself mentally, feeling the Devil try to bend the world around him, but he held it together.

He headed back to the campsite, forgetting why he had gone into the forest in the first place. When he remembered, he saw the light of the campsite fire and several of the kids up and about. Probably the gun shot had awakened them.

Joe ran toward him.

"Oh my god—what happened, Mr. Green?"

"What did I tell you kids about...good Lord...in vain?"

"Why are you holding your side like that? We heard a gun go off."

"It's...nothing." He forced a smile. "Just tripped over a rock, and...fell down is all. Landed on a sharp fallen branch, or a thorny bush, or something—nothing serious." The word 'serious' seemed to come out in slow-motion.

Thou shalt not bear false witness, a voice said much too loudly in his head.

But! he thought, *I must.* The children would not understand; they wouldn't listen to his next set of commandments if he told them what really happened.

It was for their own good—they couldn't know the truth, and they could not be involved in his battle.

Joe began trying to help him walk back, then gasped and drew back his hand, discovering the blood on his side.

Eric panicked at first, then realized the blood supported his story—pierced by a thorn or two or something of the sort. Yes, they will believe.

"Now, listen," he said, mustering up all his focus. "I want you kids to start heading back on the trail—I'll catch up to you. The Boy Scout can take the lead. Now bring a map," he said.

Someone brought a map to him.

"You will need to go here," he said to David, "and follow this." He pointed, then grabbed the compass around his neck, and was about to give it to David when he realized it had broken during his mishap. He stared at the cross and thought he saw parts of it jump beyond its boundary for a moment, needle dancing before his face. He suddenly felt cold.

He had to move quickly.

"You understand?" he asked David, and David nodded, and it appeared for a moment as if his face slid off his skull. The Devil was on his way.

"Don't worry, Mr. Green—I have a compass," David said, flashing him an encouraging grin, and Eric figured the kid had probably obtained it from Jake's bag. He was glad.

"Now, go on," he said, relieved they were in good hands, and hoping they all left immediately.

But Luz soon ran over, clearly forgetting his earlier rebuke since she couldn't stop saying: "oh my god, oh my god." Finally she said: "Maybe I can help," and ran back to her tent.

Everything became like a dream to him, the atmosphere taking on a mirage-like quality, colors twisting around him in odd dances.

Luz came back with a first aid kit, and he let her clean his wound and apply bandages.

When she looked up at him, her eyes looked hopeful.

"Mr. Green, you're right—it's not that bad, just a scratch."

"Good, now go! I'll join you soon enough." He was having trouble thinking clearly.

Half of them had already taken down their tents and

repacked themselves, ready to head off, but Luz wouldn't stop looking at him. Joe's concerned dark eyes were on him too.

"I don't understand..." Luz began.

"Oh my god, look how pale he's getting," he heard a female voice whisper. *Narine*, he thought. "He totally looks like he's dying." *Yes, definitely Narine.*

"Get the hell of here!" Eric said at last. "I have some things I need to do that I can't explain to you. Now go—the sooner the better. I'll catch up with you later."

Now, four out of the six kids were ready to go and David had even started walking ahead, Ralph not far behind, although glancing back. Bluto and Narine stayed back to watch for a bit, but turned to hurry off at the sound of heavy rustling and movement coming from the forest, like an animal galloping through.

Then Joe came over and grabbed Luz—the only one who wouldn't stop staring at him as if that was all it would take to heal him.

"You have to go, sweetheart," he said softly to her, as Joe began pulling her away.

Luz broke away from Joe's grip to head back to him, but all she said when she got to him and grabbed his hand was: "Mr. Green, please pray—please say you'll do that for me."

And he nodded.

Her mouth tilted into a smile that went way too high

on one side, then she turned around and joined the rest of her hurrying group.

Eric smiled to himself, his heart full.

The kids disappeared from view.

He lay there on his bag, praying for the kids' safety, breathing deeply.

Eric didn't know how long it had been since he heard the last sounds of the kids' presence, had no idea how far they had gotten as he enjoyed the way everything he looked at seemed to leave a trail. All he knew when he heard the disturbance in the forest nearing, was that it wasn't one of the kids returning for him.

He heard a muffled snort to his left, branches snapping ahead, and a persistent chomping sound all around. Beelzebub had finally arrived.

He waited for his final tribulation.

Then it occurred to him: why should he wait? *God helps those who help themselves.*

Surely as long as he could move, he had a chance to draw the beast away from the kids.

He peeled himself up and tried to imagine a map of the area.

If he could only get to water, he figured, maybe he could also increase his chances. Keep himself hydrated, clean out the wound—something, anything. Water always cleansed, right?

Eric gathered all his strength just as the creature

presented himself directly, its head massive, large enough to obscure the rest of its body.

Its two lower tusks coated with blood and spit gleamed like steel, snapping sporadically against its upper cluster of blood-soaked teeth.

Eric raised Jake's gun, hoping he could get it to fire. But instead it elongated, morphing into a black serpent raising itself as if preparing to strike.

Eric hurled it at the porcine beast, then burst into a run.

It seemed to him the monster took a moment to right itself before tunneling itself in his direction in chase.

Eric knew it could only be the strength of his belief, the favor of God powering him as he made his way toward water.

He leapt over a log carpeted in moss, dodged outreaching branches left and right, survival instincts taking over as he powered through the forest like a panther.

Relief flooded him as he finally reached a clearing at the edge of a large waterfall, pouring into a shimmering basin.

With the beast just about to strike, his only chance was to take a leap, and God would take it from there.

He soared through the air smiling, filled with hope for a few glorious moments before filling with wonder at having triumphed over death from venomous fangs and the stabs of a wild beast only to discover his watery savior shallow.

He felt himself dying slowly as he twitched on the rocks he landed on, watching his blood stain the water as it bathed him, the river flowing red till he had no more.

NINE

HOG WILD

As they settled themselves amongst their chosen trees to wait out the night, Luz couldn't stop thinking about Mr. Green all by himself in the dark forest. How scary and horrible it must be to wait for some animal to come crashing through, and fight alone for them like that with little hope.

What did Mr. Green ever do to anybody?

And who knew what other wild animals would do to his body by the time anyone got back to it?

Luz thought about Jake and Melanie too—both ending up in the wrong place at the wrong time, and dying for it.

What a crap shoot, she thought, remembering the way luck played with people as she watched them at the tables, her dad among them. She herself had had nothing to do with where she was born and to whom, why her sight was spared from a knife slash.

"This trip really isn't turning out very well," she said into the quiet, adjusting herself on her branch. "What if it's cursed?"

"Cursed? Really?" Bluto replied from the tree across from hers. "You're telling me you're stupid-stitious too?"

"Look, just lay off her. What the fuck did she do to you?" Joe said to her delight, and she was glad he had chosen the same tree as her, that he was so nearby.

"You watch your mouth there, lover boy. I know you wanna tap that; that's why you're so defensive of her. Slim pickings out here—although yours, not so slim."

"I'm tired of your shit, Bluto—we're all stuck here trying to figure out how to survive, and all you do is try to fuck with people. You ran Melanie off with your clever shit and now the last adult is probably dead, and you're still picking on people. Like Mr. Green said, you just waste energy fighting. If we're gonna get through this, it's gotta be together."

"Oh, kumbaya. You're really taking advice from someone who's probably rotting back there right now?" Bluto shot back.

Luz's eyes filled with tears. The image was too real: Mr. Green's cold body curdling to rot.

She felt a different quality to the silence among them —as if Bluto had finally gone too far for all of them.

Luz looked over at Narine in the branch above him. Her face was illuminated by the flashlight she held, and

Luz noticed she indeed looked bothered by Bluto's comment.

She looked over at the others in their own tree.

Both Ralph and David were looking away—Ralph's head down, David looking ahead—as if in their own worlds.

Get it together, she told herself. *You've seen worse.*

———

AS DAYLIGHT BEGAN to peek over the horizon, they made their way out of the trees, gathering up their backpacks at the bases. Once David started walking, they followed him.

Luz wondered what the others were thinking, what kept them quiet the few hours they waited in the trees, and what kept them quiet now. Were they also envisioning their family members and the warm beds they had left behind? Regretting the deeds that brought them here at this horrible time? About the future? About Melanie and Jake? About Mr. Green?

Half an hour passed in silence before Luz decided to speak.

"How much longer do you think we have? *If* we get out?"

Bluto let out a heavy sigh. "Are you ever optimistic about anything? You're like that dude Eeyore on Winnie the Pooh. Didn't you hear Huntsman at the beginning?" Bluto said.

"Yeah, attitude is everything," Narine said. "You won't get out of here alive with *that* attitude."

"But sometimes, it's just luck."

"Oh, Christ—are we really having a philosophical conversation right now? Seriously?"

Luz was caught off guard by David's curt reply, yet it fortified her somewhat. "Okay, well then how about a practical one: you sure you know where the hell you're going? 'Cause according to what Mr. Green said, we were supposed to hit some springs and then we'd be about two hours away from the main trails. We haven't even stopped or anything since...since we left him back there. We should at least be able to see something familiar by now."

"Look, I know where I'm going, okay?"

Narine stopped dead in her tracks.

Everyone stopped to look at her.

"I think I remember seeing *that* before," she said, pointing to a mossy log beyond the bushes.

Everyone's eyes went to David's, and all except David and Ralph stopped walking.

"I thought you said you knew where you were going," Bluto said in an accusatory tone.

David brushed away his words.

"I do. We're going in the right direction, you guys, I swear."

"Really? Then why does this tree look familiar?" Bluto asked. "Why does it feel like we've passed that bush right there already?"

"It's daytime," David said, spacing out his words as if talking to a group of slow kids. "You think you can really tell what things look like now compared to last night? Besides, it's a forest—of course some parts of it look familiar; it's just a bunch of bushes and moss and shit, and sometimes, there's more than one of the same bush. You really think there's only one fallen tree in a wilderness like this?"

"Probably not," Narine said, "but not one next to that berry bush like that. And look at the way it's angled—I remember the way the light from my flashlight hit it. And see there? Those big white mushrooms over there..."

Most of the group stared at David skeptically and he halted his steps at last, Ralph almost running into him.

"Look, if you guys don't trust me and have a problem with the way we're going, I suggest you go on and head off where you think you should go."

"I think we should go this way," Luz said, pointing. Her gut had already told her something didn't feel right, that David was wrong.

"Based on what?" Bluto said, punctuating every word with disgust despite having expressed skepticism himself.

"I don't know—it just seems the way we came from yesterday."

"Well, I think it's this way," Narine said, pointing in a different direction, about forty-five degrees away from her estimation.

Joe sighed, Bluto shook his head, and Luz had a feeling they were all thinking the same thing. It was obvious what would come next.

Bluto verbalized her suspicion. "Let's just split up," he said. "This is ridiculous."

"Why would we do that? There's strength in numbers, right? Everyone knows that," Joe said.

"Obviously, we're just slowing each other down. Besides, I'm kind of feeling Narine in that direction. And anyway, I don't want to be around that fat, whiny bitch, and I certainly don't want to be tempted to kick the shit out of your worthless ass all day. Mama's boy. Or should I say, grandmama's boy? Oh, by the way—look what I found." Bluto produced a photo of an elderly, smiling black woman, holding the photo up for a moment before preparing his fingers as if to rip it.

Joe's face filled with rage, and he lunged at Bluto, grabbing his face, every one of his ten fingers finding a snug home in and around Bluto's dense skull—his jaw, his cheeks, eyes and temples all in a vice grip.

Bluto cried out in a deep roar as if to scare the clinch away, flailing his fists and drumming against Joe's body and arms.

Joe seemed to hear and feel nothing, swinging the

enormous man-child around, causing Bluto to stumble. Then Joe used the falling momentum to spin Bluto to the ground.

Bluto got up quickly, but the immense power Joe had displayed over him seemed to give him pause.

"What the hell was that? You can't fight like a man?" Bluto protested, panting, not bothering to stop Joe from recovering the photo.

"Stop!" David's voice rang out with stunning command, grabbing everyone's attention. Bluto looked relieved at the interruption. "Just get into groups of people who don't want to kill each other," David continued. "Can we all find at least one person to go with?"

"Well, I'm with Luz," Joe said, closing in on her side so that their arms touched.

"Surprise, surprise," Bluto said.

"Like you're one to talk," Joe said as Narine sided up to him.

Ralph looked at David, who wasn't looking at anyone.

"I'll just keep going with him," Ralph said, though it was obvious he had no choice since Bluto had already given Ralph a look that said he was not welcome.

Luz was glad Joe had decided to come with her; he had been the only one who had been nice to her. Besides, she didn't quite trust the other two boys—something about David rubbed her the wrong way, and Ralph didn't seem to have much of a mind of his own out here.

She was happy Joe trusted her, and even if it wasn't trust, she was glad for his friendship.

She put her hand on her belly then quickly moved it, looking around to see if anyone had caught the movement, but Bluto and Narine were too busy deciding their new route, while David and Ralph had already headed out on their own without another word.

Joe had set down his backpack to pull out his map. He looked at it for a few seconds, then jammed it back in.

"I don't even know why I bothered to do that—I don't know where we are or anything."

They both heard Narine giggle and turned toward her.

She and Bluto were also studying a map, and although she wasn't looking at them now, they were both sure the giggle had been at their expense.

"Don't worry about them, Luz—we'll find our way." He nudged her from looking in their direction. "Let's just start going the way you said earlier."

Backpacks in place, they set out on her hunch.

———

WORRY SURGED through Narine once she and Bluto were alone—she hadn't realized how much of a difference traveling in a pack made, how much more comfortable and safe she had felt. Now, with just the two of them, she felt more vulnerable to any wild animal, despite Bluto's huge size which was why she had chosen him to begin with.

He was the epitome of the advice Jake had given when it came to facing off with some wild animals—make yourself appear bigger than they are. Bluto didn't have to fake it at all—surely he dwarfed anything out here—except maybe a bear or that giant pig.

Still, as long as Bluto was with her, she had a better chance. Bluto could reach things, break things, and maybe even carry her on his back if needed. He could probably punch that monster pig in the face and send it flying. Plus, he wasn't afraid of anything.

To top it off, he had that bad-ass knife. In the right hands, it could really do some damage, and Bluto had some very large hands; he would be her bodyguard.

He was just like the rest—one smile, and they thought you wanted them, would do anything to make sure you liked them if they thought they could get something from you.

"So you're good with that knife?" she asked him slyly.

The look on his face said he had caught her drift. "We'll see when it's time to use it—but yeah, I can definitely wield this thing."

Narine smiled. "Good."

He smiled back, his eyes dancing with hope.

Sucker.

"THAT REALLY WAS A CIRCLE, wasn't it?" Ralph asked David, whose look remained impassive. "You don't like anybody here—that's why. You wanted everyone to split up. You don't want to be around any of them, and you wanted them to doubt you. You planned that whole thing somehow, so you can get out of here fast without the extra weight."

Ralph knew if he was right, then they were pretty much back at the beginning, with at least six hours to go before they reached where the van had dropped them off.

David didn't answer.

"Look, I came with you because I know you know the right way out of here."

David still didn't say anything, but Ralph didn't care. He could tell—if there was one person who knew how to survive this thing with smarts on top of wilderness knowledge, it was this guy.

He felt safe with his decision—although it was hardly much of a decision after Bluto made it clear he didn't want anything to do with him, and that sort of slutty-looking girl had decided to be with him.

Sure, he could've joined Joe and Luz, but Joe was so young and that girl, Luz, only looked like a liability—a bit emotional and kind of chubby—probably couldn't move very well. Joe even had to help her get up their tree earlier, unlike the rest of them who were able to climb on their own. Ultimately, Ralph didn't trust the youngest member's choice—some girl making a guess who seemed to be more a hindrance than anything.

Not only did David seem smart, he had been a Boy Scout. He had even ventured off on his own at least twice since they had come here, and nothing had happened to him.

On top of everything else, Ralph had seen some of what David had palmed when they were ransacking Jake's backpack that the other group members probably missed. While Joe and Bluto were busy arguing and fighting over that sick knife, David had been so fast, he had slipped a number of objects from Jake's backpack to his own.

Ralph wasn't sure what they all were, but he caught sight of a few very useful looking items, including something electronic—probably a GPS of some sort. He caught the words "pocket chainsaw" and he had no idea what that was, but it sounded awesome. And useful. Plus, he got a few other things that really caught Ralph's eye—some fire-starters.

It only made sense for Ralph to go with the most prepared person—he himself had only managed to grab a pack of peanuts and a lighter.

Even Luz had made out better than him—although when she first grabbed the first aid kit, Bluto yanked it from her. Luckily for her, he was soon distracted by fighting over that knife with Joe, and Luz managed to sneak the first aid kit back from him amongst a few other things.

Ralph wondered what else he had missed at the beginning of that fight, although near the end of it, he saw Narine grab some food bars. After Bluto won, Joe took a few of the leftovers: snare wire, a whistle. Ralph couldn't help wondering: a whistle? What could they possibly do with a whistle but draw the attention of the wrong creature? Still, he understood the logic of leaving nothing behind—you never knew what could come in handy, and when.

Ralph could have sworn he had seen a more detailed map too, but didn't see where that had gone to. Only later did he realize David had managed to swipe that as well.

Everything pointed to David being his best chance.

TEN

SWEATING LIKE A PIG

"**W**hat kind of animals are gonna be out there?" Joe had asked Jake as they began their hike into the wilderness. And he had been told: squirrels, skunks and raccoons. Snakes and lizards. Salamanders and toads. Maybe elk. Rabbits and possums. Coyotes, porcupines and bats. Wild cats, perhaps.

Will bears be out there? he had wondered, then asked aloud, and he had been told bears lived there, but it was unlikely the group would encounter one.

Nobody had said a thing about man-eating pigs.

Joe was used to seeing dogs and rats. Pigeons, and cats. Cockroaches, too. Plus ants and spiders. Those were the animals that populated his building, his neighborhood, his life. Birds and insects, canines and felines. That was it.

Other than those, he had caught glimpses of other creatures on cartoons, or otherwise heard of the ones Jake talked about, and those that lived in zoos—he knew about those.

He had never been to a zoo—had never, in fact, been outside of where he now lived with all the relatives in his life: his mom. He had never met anyone from his dad's side, his grandfather was dead, and his mother's estranged sisters were irrelevant.

He hardly went anywhere—home, school, church. That was it. His whole life fit into five square miles.

And now here he was, a couple thousand miles away from home, and actually seeing some of the animals he had seen on television in front of him.

To see some of the creatures in real life made him almost forget about the danger around him, the death behind—and perhaps ahead of—him.

How could he think of death when there, right there, was a real life rabbit? So cute, so unlike its cartoon version —although he didn't really expect to see a tall, grey, smart-aleck bunny with unnaturally large eyes chewing on a carrot. But to see the small and swift, shy, snuggly version in its very real dumb animal state teased a grin from him.

Luz even had to hold him back from following a skunk, which he hadn't realized he was about to do until he felt her hand on his chest to stop him.

"Don't scare it," she had said. "You don't want to smell that shit it lets out when bothered."

Joe wasn't sure how it worked—did it spray you in the

face? Was it like a fart that spread through the air and then stung your eyes? He wasn't sure he wanted to find out, so he let it go. But boy was it beautiful—essentially a larger, furrier, cuddly-looking rat with glossy black fur and a beautiful white streak from head to bushy tail.

Even the thought of running into deer fascinated him. He vaguely remembered seeing the movie *Bambi* when he was younger, although he hadn't seen the whole thing—his mom told him he had burst into tears and was inconsolable and inattentive once Bambi's mom disappeared.

And now there she was! Scaring them out of their wits at first when they spotted her.

She was so beautiful, startled by them; everything to him—so, so beautiful.

———

"So how'd you get your scar?"

Joe had noticed as soon as their faces were close enough that the shimmery thing he had once mistaken for a tear on Luz's face was actually ripped skin healed.

"Stabbed," she said, and Joe felt his heart dive.

"My ex-boyfriend, when I broke up with him, slashed me across the face and said I would always belong to him and no one else would want me."

"You don't believe that, do you?"

Luz shrugged, then looked down. She seemed to be

struggling with something, and when she looked up again, her eyes were glassy. "Look, I'm sorry about getting emotional," she said. "It's just...I can't believe I'm about to say this, but you should know since we're gonna be sticking together. Nobody else knows, and I didn't plan on telling anyone since we were only gonna be here a few weeks." She put her hand on her belly. "I'm pregnant," she said. "I don't know how far along—maybe a few months."

"You're what?" Joe immediately looked down at her stomach as if he could tell the truth of her statement there. "No one? Not even the father knows?"

Luz shook her head. "Not even my parents," she said. "Just you and me."

Joe didn't understand it. Wouldn't someone in her life notice a difference?

He realized the question must have shown on his face, since she went on to say:

"I've always been sort of a big girl—at least compared to the girls on TV. I'm pretty normal-sized in my neighborhood, and don't exactly stand out at school. According to what I see around in general, I'm pretty much average American-sized." She looked away. "Even if I had gained a lot of weight, no one would notice. No one would probably notice if I started to grow a third breast unless it was holding a gun."

Joe's urge to laugh was strangled by pity. How was it she had no one paying attention to her?

"What are you going to do?" he asked. "And why would you come on a wilderness hike like this?"

"I didn't have a choice—it was this or get kicked out. Besides, I don't think this will hurt the baby—unless that monster gets me or something."

"Yeah, or you fall or...I don't know—it just seems like a dangerous place for a baby to be—even an unborn one."

Luz caressed her belly, still looking away.

"So what are you going to do when we get back?"

"Honestly, I don't know. I've been thinking maybe adoption..."

"But you're definitely going to keep it? I mean, are you thinking about..."

Luz shook her head vigorously. "Abortion? Are you crazy? If my parents ever found out, they'd kill me. And anyway, I'm still a Catholic girl—I don't believe in abortion like that; I can't imagine killing my baby."

Joe was quiet for a few moments.

"What would you name it if it's a girl?"

Luz seemed to think for a minute. Then she smiled. "Lucia," she said.

"And if it's a boy?"

"I don't know—I don't have any pet boy names like that, you know? I guess I always imagined I would have a girl."

"But what if you have twins?"

She shoved him playfully. "Don't say that—it would be

so hard to give them away. But there's no way I could keep them, no way I could afford to take care of them. A church collection can't help with that." Her smile was sad. Then it disappeared completely. "You know, my mom already said she wouldn't bother helping me with any bastard kids—especially around this age—and my grandmother hates my ex. And anyway, I probably won't name the baby, not if it's going off to a new family. What's the point?"

Joe felt it was time to change the subject. "How come you don't go by your first name? I don't know much Spanish, but I sure know Luz ain't short for Maria."

Luz laughed. "No, I just make everyone call me Luz because I think it's prettier. It means 'light.' And my middle name is Luz, so using it isn't all that crazy."

"Oh. Well, why didn't you just say that?"

"Because it's more about what it means than it just happening to be my middle name, you know?"

Joe shrugged. "I guess." Then he remembered something she had said earlier. "So what did you really do to get here? And what did your family say to get you to agree to this?" he asked.

Luz sighed deeply. "I brought shame on the family for becoming nothing but a *cholita*," she said. "My name got entered into this gang database, and the cops sent my family a letter about it. My mom and grandma were so disappointed in me and I felt bad, you know? I mean, I'm not even in a gang, but my association with

Emilio...anyway, like they tell me 'you lie down with dogs, you wake up with fleas,' so I just took responsibility; I knew they just wanted to help me even though they basically said if I didn't take action, they'd kick me out. They thought this program would help.

"They love me, I know that—and they want to make sure I stay alive. Being around Emilio was dangerous, and they just want me to have a second chance, a better shot at life—even without knowing about the baby. I mean, I probably would've done this anyway, to make them happy, but this was especially for my baby, despite the risk. My ex-boyfriend might come back and try to kill me, you know? And this retreat gives me some time away from home. Emilio can't get me here, and maybe time will help him cool off or move on. Plus, I have time to think, figure out what's best for her. Yes, it's a her, I'm sure of it." She paused a moment. "You know, I even dream about her."

"You already love her, don't you?"

"Of course I do—it's my baby! She's mine and she hasn't done anything to deserve this. She still has a shot— even if I don't—and I'll do everything it takes to keep her alive and safe. Anyway, what about you? What was the deal about the robbery?"

He shook his head. "I don't even know how to hold a gun. Anyway, a week after my grandmother's funeral, I went to the corner store with my friends. I had no idea what they had planned. One of them pulled out a gun, then shouted at me to grab the store owner to stop him from grabbing his. I saw the look on Mr. Han's face, then did what he said." He let out a breath, remembering.

Death was no longer a faraway, hardly glimpsed possibility to him after having witnessed his grandmother's death. Luckily, he was faster and stronger than Mr. Han, and he leapt over the counter, grabbed him, then dragged him away from the low shelf where the butt of a gun was visible, and while holding on to him, his friend Javier went to the cash register and emptied it.

Mr. Han had no chance fighting against his grip, and Joe let him go only when the boys said, "Let's go!" and ran out of the store.

Once Joe released him, they both ran, but in opposite directions. Joe didn't bother to see if Mr. Han had gone for his weapon or the phone.

"This keeps me out of jail...well, juvie anyway. The court offered alternative sentencing. If I finish the camp, no conviction, no record or anything. Plus, this sounded kinda fun—I never got to leave my city before—barely left my neighborhood. I mean, it's like a cool adventure I get to go on to erase my crime—doesn't get much better than that. I've never been camping before. And someone actually paying for me to go, trying to help me out—that means something, you know? Not too many show that kind of faith: my mom, my grandmother, and even that store owner, who agreed to this. This whole thing was a win-win for me; far as I know, I don't even owe anything after this—no money, that is."

"So what are *you* going to do when we get out of here?"

Joe shook his head. "I don't know. Find out who my Secret Santa was? Maybe my mom will tell me then."

"What do you mean?"

"Well, we're not exactly from Beverly Hills either, so there's no way my family could have sent me on this retreat—not even if someone had taken up a collection. I heard this thing cost thousands. Anyway, someone put up the money."

"Your dad maybe?"

Joe couldn't look at her. "My dad died when I was two —some subway train accident; my mom doesn't like to talk about it. Anyway, at first, my mom and I thought this camp was a lost cause. Then one day, she told me she got the money. I asked her from who 'cause I know she didn't just bring home some check worth thousands—she's a court clerk; I don't think they make that much money—at least, she's always telling me money doesn't grow on trees. Anyway, she started playing cute and said she couldn't tell me yet. All she could say was that he had a favor to ask of me when all this was done."

"So what is it? What's the big favor?"

"Hell if I know. I got really confused when she mentioned it was a 'he.' I had guessed up to that point that maybe my grandmother left something in her will or something."

"When did your grandmother die?"

Joe let out another breath.

If his grandmother had been around that day, maybe he wouldn't have gotten involved in the robbery.

Joe knew he lived in a bad neighborhood, but never thought two old ladies walking back from the corner store could get caught in a spray of careless bullets.

The worst part was that he knew who was behind it—one of the neighborhood drug dealers. The guy's crew had been trying to get somebody who had ratted them out to the cops for something else, and in their tunnel vision, it didn't matter who had gotten in the way or had the bad luck of being on the block the same time as their target, whether it was a little girl or an old, outspoken, but harmless woman.

There were two fatalities that day—a seven-year-old girl who had been found alive, bleeding, still holding one end of her jump rope but died later at a hospital, and his grandmother, who had died at the scene.

His grandmother's friend had survived—hadn't even caught a single bullet even though she was walking right next to his grandmother. And the boy the drug dealer's goons had gone after had taken several bullets but lived.

Joe had been in his room at the time and ran to his

window at the sound of the shots without thinking, and witnessed the scene.

Joe fought against the lump in his throat.

"Not long before I had to pack up and come here. She got caught in a drive-by walking back to our house with her friend. Little girl got hit too."

Luz hung her head, seeming embarrassed for having brought it up. "I'm sorry," she said.

"It's not your fault, but thanks. The camp leader let me bring that book here with her picture in it—the one Bluto was messing with—so I kind of still have her with me."

Joey is a good boy, he once overheard her telling a friend of hers who had come to visit. *If he makes it out of this shithole alive and gets to eighteen, he'll make something of himself.*

She had been sitting there, knitting scarves with her friend, while he was doing his homework in the other room —although he would never admit that part to his friends.

He always pretended he didn't care about school with them. They had no idea he was getting As and Bs—they thought he was flunking out, soon to join them. But he had other plans—he was going to make his grandmother proud.

"Anyway, as far as other family, my mom just has two sisters—one older, one younger—who I've never seen. The older one just kind of disappeared to make her own life and didn't really keep in touch with the family—I heard she's a doctor. The younger one—no one really mentions her; everyone's way too embarrassed to have anything to do with her."

"Why is that?"

Joe shrugged. "They never really told me any details, but from what I heard, and the way they turn up their mouths when talking about her, I figure she's probably a coke-head prostitute. I'm just guessing, but why else would no one want to claim her? Has to be pretty extreme. Anyway, like I said, I can't really imagine who would front that kind of money for me and why, and I know my mom didn't just sell me to some old pedophile dude." Joe paused. Then it hit him. "You know what? There's this guy who owns a gym who asked me about sports before—if I ever thought about maybe getting professionally involved. I guess it might be him. I told him I hadn't really thought about anything like that, and he just kept looking at me like —I don't know, it was almost like he had dollar signs in his eyes. He told me I should think about it. That he'd give me a free boxing lesson so I could see how I liked it. I never took him up on it. I bet he wants me to train with him."

"So you'll take him up on it?"

"I don't think I have a choice. I think by accepting his money, I have to go ahead and give it a shot."

They walked on in silence.

Joe wasn't sure how much time had passed with both

of them in their own heads, and he didn't know what Luz was thinking about, but all his thoughts had to do with her. He knew right then that he had a crush.

He hadn't had a crush in a while—not since he was eight years old and one of his neighbors started having a little girl about his age visit. She was apparently just there for the summer, which he was brokenhearted to find out once the end of August came.

And now here he was, probably in a fight for his life, and all he could think about was what it would be like to kiss the girl next to him.

He wanted to brush his finger against the scar under her eye to see what it felt like, brush his lips against hers to see what they felt like.

He wondered how her body would feel pressed against his.

Joe had never kissed a girl, and it didn't matter that this girl next to him was carrying a child, and probably still a flame for her ex.

When he noticed her breathing seemed labored, he suggested they stop.

She insisted they go on. "Please don't make me feel like a burden," she said, her eyes pleading, but there was no way he would force her to go on, especially knowing what he now knew about her.

He had no idea how much longer they had to go, so if

she needed a rest, they would take one. Besides, it was daylight—he could keep an eye on her easily.

"I'll look out," he said. "Take as long as you need."

She looked skeptical but didn't put up a fight as he started setting up her tent.

"I'll use mine as a weapon if I have to," he said, grinning. And he meant it.

Luz smiled gratefully at him before disappearing into her tent.

Joe looked forward to the animal-watching ahead of him.

———

Luz FELT her brain scrambling from overstimulation. There were just too many sounds, and almost all of them she had no clue what was making them, and it was making her crazy.

If Jake had been there, maybe he would have been able to explain why that particular sound—which might have come from a bird—was, as if the animal were being stabbed. And that one—it sounded like some kind of owl, but what owl was awake in the daytime? She had heard they were nocturnal.

Still, Luz was glad to hear rather than see the owl—owls gave her the creeps: those large, intelligent, sometimes human-looking eyes. There was something a bit too familiar about them, yet it made no sense that they should be familiar—she had never lived around them. They seemed too present, too direct in their look. Too knowing. What was it they knew? And who were they watching, or keeping an eye out for? Who? Who?

And those other animals, making sounds like very audible breaths. Sometimes high-pitched sounds alternating with exhalations, like a large, invisible animal sleeping on its back. Rapid musical breaths, snores.

And the insects wouldn't shut up—the grasshoppers, crickets, whatever the hell they were.

Too many unknowns, too many eyes, too many living spirits surrounding them with unknown intents and habits. Too many shadows on her tent.

Even after living in a gang-infested neighborhood with gun-toting neighbors, friends and enemies, having had her ex-boyfriend attack her with a knife, having brawled with brutish girls who threatened her life, and having no doubt they meant it, being out here in the wilderness was much worse.

She had never felt so unsafe in her life. She could hardly sleep! Only knowing Joe was near was the slightest comfort. And when she finally managed to shut her eyes and think about her room at home to take her mind off of all the possible silently approaching menaces, her visions began with wild images of animals intent on tormenting her, if not outright attacking her—pterodactyls descending onto her tent, tigers trying to paw their way in, bears slapping it around. A pair of blue-black beetles planning to clamp onto her big toes with sharp pincers, a swarm of red ants approaching over a dirt hill aiming to cover her and inject their poison, stinging her relentlessly. Antlered deer ripping her tent apart to make sure she was more vulnerable to approaching porcupines, rolling toward her. Poison ivy crawling around trees and slowly extending its way toward her to wrap her in its leaves.

Fevered dreams causing her to spring up like a rat trap, sweating like a pig.

ELEVEN

WALLOWING IN MUD

Bluto was still flicking his flashlight about in a way that made Narine feel she was about to have an epileptic seizure. She had to get her mind off the twitchy movement—her eyes started following it like a dog following a strip of bacon treat dangling back and forth from teasing hands.

Why did he still have it out anyway, instead of that knife he had gotten?

"So you had a pretty good voice back there, when you sang to Melanie."

Narine thought she saw a halt in Bluto's step as the flashlight steadied itself.

She almost regretted her choice of silence-breaker, and wondered if Bluto felt bad at all for what he had said to Melanie; for all they knew, it was because of him she was dead.

"Shit, I can sing better than that—that was a joke."

"Do you sing in school?"

He shook his head vigorously. "Of course not."

"What do you mean 'of course not'?"

"What would I look like singing in some glee club or something? I have a reputation to protect."

"What the hell are you talking about? You think people will suddenly stop being afraid of you? That you'll, like, shrink in front of their eyes?"

He shrugged.

"Are you crazy, Bluto? You're still a huge guy—I doubt anyone would mess with you just because they found out you could sing. And anyway, you shouldn't care about what people think. You only let them stop you from being happy. And then they win without you even starting the race. That's just stupid. If you want to sing, you should sing."

"Life ain't that simple, princess," he said.

"Well, it looks like it to me. I mean, who are you really afraid of? The way it sounds like you run that school, no one would be dumb enough to mess with you, even if you randomly broke out into a solo every now and then."

"Yeah, but then I'd get kicked out for sure the next time I get in trouble for beating someone up—which I know I'd have to do because, trust me, at least one person would have some smart-ass thing to say. I can't do that; I just can't give anyone a reason to mess with me again. I can't risk kicking someone else's ass in that school."

She let a few seconds pass. "Seems to me there's more to the story. What's the deal? And don't worry—I won't tell anyone, I promise. I mean, who am I gonna tell?"

He seemed to think about it for a moment, a war with himself reflecting on his face. She even thought she saw a flash of pain.

"It's my dad," he said at last, then stopped, like he was rethinking confiding in her. "There's no way my dad would accept me joining some chorus," he continued.

"Okay," she said slowly. "I...guess I can understand that." She knew her tone said the opposite. It got the desired effect.

"Look, I've got to do what it takes to keep my dad happy. Otherwise..." He stopped again. "Otherwise, my sister might suffer."

Narine suddenly changed her mind about pushing for more information; where he was going sounded too deep; she had gotten a creepy feeling about the story behind his words.

Time to change the subject.

"So, how do you think the others are making out?" Narine asked.

"Who gives a fuck?"

Narine decided to stay silent.

"They're probably okay for at least the first day—I mean, we haven't come across their bodies yet or anything."

Narine remained silent.

"What, you worried about them?"

Finally, she decided to speak. "I just think—I don't know, I guess I think we should have stayed together. Pooled our resources, you know?"

"What, let our powers combine?" Bluto rolled his eyes. "I mean, I bet that cow got all the granola bars," he began. "If we were together, maybe she'd share. But I can't believe you're back to that. I mean, did you get a load of that knife I got? Trust me, we're good."

But didn't Jake at least have a knife on him? And he wasn't exactly good. Nothing Jake had had was enough.

Narine realized she had gotten entangled in her thoughts only when Bluto spoke again, jarring her out of them.

She wondered at how all of a sudden he seemed more interested in what she had to say in general—perhaps, like her, preferring petty chat in the wilderness to being a silent prisoner of it.

"So your parents sent you here for something besides being self-...uh, hot and sexy—what was it? Had to be something criminal."

"I don't want to talk about it," Narine said.

"Come on, what the hell else are we gonna talk about

out here? Do you really want to just concentrate on looking out for that breast...*beast* and being scared at every little rustle? What difference does it make?"

She still didn't respond, employing once again the trick she had learned early: silent treatments usually got more out of people than prodding them.

"Okay, I'll tell you what I did—although I know you think it's obvious. So people call me a bully, sure—first kid I picked on and beat up was eight. But so was I—I just happened to be a lot bigger than him. I took his lunch for the day. He had a cookie I wanted, and I hadn't had a cookie since my mom died, and my dad never bothered to try to make them; she'd died a few months before this incident, actually—right before I turned eight. Anyway, I didn't beat up anyone else for a while, although whenever I looked at that kid I beat up a certain way, he just offered me his cookie.

"The first time I actually got in trouble for bullying I was ten. This time, the kid didn't have anything I wanted. I just needed some kind of punching bag, I guess, and he looked like a good target. My dad had locked me out of the house the night before, and I had to sleep in our back yard, so I guess you could say I woke up on the wrong side of the flowerbed."

"Wait, what?" Narine paused to look at him to see if he was serious.

"He did stuff like that sometimes," Bluto said,

continuing to walk. She had no choice but to do the same although his indifference bothered her; she couldn't imagine any of her parents doing anything like that to her.

"That was a one-time thing, right? I mean, you know that's not normal?"

Bluto looked at her. "It's normal raising a boy, I think. To make him a man. Can't do stuff like that with girls. It helped toughen me up. You know, one time—I was about nine—my dad put out some dog food for me instead of making dinner."

"But that's horrible!"

Bluto seemed surprised at her exclamation.

"It's tough being a single dad all of a sudden like that. Raising a boy like me and a little girl all on his own. He probably only did that because he was really tired that night—too tired to even try anything. Probably getting a little old, too—bad eyes, I guess. Maybe he thought it was a can of tuna—I don't know."

"But still, that's..."

"He was doing his best. And he always used force for a reason. It made me tough, and taught me the value of a good smack. I was asking for it—getting in fights all the time, making him use his work time to hear some parent or teacher bitch and moan about their pathetic kid and what I'd done. And you see these?" He pointed out some scars on his arm.

"What are those?" she asked, not sure she wanted to know the answer.

"Punishment," he said. "For fuckin' up. Dad would push his cigarettes into my skin to put them out on days the school called our house. Don't look at me like that—he was just helping me remember the rules—not like I didn't know. I just...I couldn't help myself sometimes. He needed a break, I think. Sometimes dad wouldn't even come home till, like, after eight or nine at night. I didn't mind though; I could do whatever I wanted when he was gone. Take a minute to watch some TV or something, instead of pretending like I'm studying or reading some book he think's gonna help me in life. I get to...I don't know—just be a kid. Anyway, I didn't just beat people up for kicks—sometimes it was to take their lunch money 'cause I didn't have any; I had to eat somehow. Plus, I had to feed my little sister. I usually have a reason.

"This one time, I beat up this guy who was harassing a girl I liked, and you know what this ungrateful bitch did? Went to his side, picked him up and gave me a look. Me! Like I was the one who called out all those nasty things to her. Constantly asked her to go out with me. Kept trying to sit next to her at lunch, making eyes at her. I mean, she'd roll her eyes, and every now and then scream out: 'would you just leave me alone?' to this guy, but now that I had taken care of her problem, I wasn't good enough for her either; she was mad at me for doing what it was obvious she needed someone to do for her—stop that perv from bugging her. Sure, I wanted to get with her too, but you didn't see me shouting shit out to her. I was a gentleman, and that was the thanks I got. She practically spat at me that I was a brute, a nasty bully who liked to pick on smaller, weaker people. I mean, that was damned obvious —she clearly wasn't the brightest bitch, but I thought she was cute. Not after that nonsense, though."

"So, not exactly popular with the ladies at your school, huh?" Narine said. *Not many of them go for the stomping Goliath like you?* she didn't say; instead, she gave him a sympathetic smile, making sure to open her eyes a bit, to project to him she was trustworthy, that *she* liked him.

Seemingly encouraged by her look, he went on, but looked down.

"Most of them hardly looked at me. Drooled over shits like Tom Wilson."

"Who was...?"

"On the football team just like me. But he was blond. Muscular. They tend to go for guys like that who are"—he distorted his face in feminine mockery—"sooo cute."

"But you went for girls who were 'sooo cute' too, right? I mean, did you go for a girl...like you?"

He scowled. "No way! What, like Madge Brennan?" He was clearly disgusted. Then, he seemed to remember she had no idea who he was referring to. "Madge is big like me, if that's what you meant. But she's a big old fat pig with greasy hair and glasses—who the hell would want that? Look, I'm no four eyes, and guys are supposed to be big. Madge is a freak. Nobody wants a freak."

Then, just like that, his confessional was over.

Narine couldn't help sizing him up then, realizing he was just a boy. It was so strange to think of this six-foot-tall guy that way, but he hadn't even started growing facial hair yet. And he certainly didn't see himself as a man yet either, not honestly.

The revelation blew her mind. He was sixteen—older than her by a year—and she thought of him as a kid. They were all just kids.

Her parents didn't try to force her to grow up—she did that on her own. She had wanted to hurry up and be allowed to be as pretty and sexy as she wanted.

She suddenly felt compelled to tell her own story.

"I got arrested for prostitution; they caught me in the mall. My parents don't have any idea though—how many relationships I've been in to get the things I want. Anyway, they were pretty horrified to find out about just that one and it was just a blow-job that time. My mom even started asking me if that was really how I'd gotten some of the things I had. Stupid bitch believed the shit I told her before—about getting hand-me-downs from rich friends and stuff like that. Anyway, when they caught me, my mom threatened to send me to some Catholic school—girls only!—and my dad just stood there.

"I thought about running away, but my guy friends have trouble housing me. I tried it once, and after paying for two nights in a hotel, this one guy crapped out on me and said I should go back home to my mommy. He had never said anything like that before! You can't depend on any of those assholes, that's for sure—I learned that quick. Get what you can from them, and split before they get tired of you. That way, you leave them maybe wanting more in the future because they didn't get to do the dumping, and you can maybe still use them in the future. It's foolproof—people have trouble getting over not being wanted by someone, even if they didn't want the person that much to begin with. It's all mental.

"Anyway, I didn't want to risk being out there unprotected like that; I'd rather have my own room with all my stuff, safe under my parents, unfortunately. I don't have enough money to go on my own yet—maybe rent for, like, a year or something. And then what? Who'll hire a fifteen year old? A fast food restaurant or a pimp, that's who. And I am *not* going down like that; my parents have a college fund for me and everything. No way I'm walking away from all that free money.

"My parents are lame, but they take care of me. And

there's no way I'm going to some shitty boy-less Catholic private school. If this is what keeps my game going, I'll do it. I only have like two years left with those lame-o's anyway. I can do that. Gives me more time to collect before I go on my own. Hopefully, by then I'll have made my way up to a car—I've been thinking a red Ferrari. I'm pretty sure I can get one of those old desperate guys to get it for me—I just need to figure out a place to keep it. For some reason, guys like giving stuff rather than money outright. I mean, they'd rather get me a thousand-dollar purse instead of just giving me, like, five hundred dollars cash. Isn't that weird? They'd rather spend more on stuff, and believe me, I've tried just getting the money. The most I've gotten directly was three hundred dollars. I was so disappointed. So I just ask for stuff. Six-hundred dollar shoes, no problem! A few nights in a five-star hotel with room-service order freedom, no biggie. But a couple hundred dollars in cold hard cash—oh no, that's not cool. I guess it makes them feel like they're paying for it." She rolled her eyes. "It's so dumb. One way or another, they pay for it. Whatever. I still get what I want out of the deal."

After a few seconds, all Bluto said was: "Wow. Gotta say though, I was expecting something like that."

"Well, I've always looked older than I am—since I was ten anyway. I had just a B-cup then. But otherwise, my body wasn't that different. Guys started acting weird toward me since then. Even really old gross ones. But eventually I learned to turn it to my advantage."

She smiled up at him, but he didn't smile back; in fact, he had something that looked like pity in his eyes.

"I'm sorry," he said.

And for some reason, she wanted to punch him in the face. She also felt sad somehow, and couldn't understand it.

He was really dumb was all—he should have been congratulating her instead of treating her like some hospital patient who just found out they had cancer.

How dare he pity her?

Her eyes watered in anger she was so offended.

She wanted to open her mouth and reproach him for his stupidity, his nearsightedness, but felt if she did, there was a chance she might sob instead.

She kept her eyes ahead of her as they continued the trek silently.

"So what are you gonna do later?" Bluto asked, breaking the silence. "Are you planning on being a pro forever or will you go to college or...I don't know, become a beautician or something?"

Narine's anger faded to amusement. "A beautician?" She laughed.

Bluto's face turned red. "Well, you know, you're all into that stuff, right? And anyway, my mom was a beautician, so I don't see what's so wrong with that."

Narine stopped laughing. "Well, I'm definitely not working in some liquor store like my loser mom. I mean, you'd think my parents were poor, looking at them—they won't get a new car or anything—but they get us all the stuff we need, and we live in a nice place, so I know they can afford to get more, and look better. Anyway, I just kind of figured I'd marry some rich guy and never have to do anything but shop, you know?"

This time, Bluto laughed. "You mean your ambition really is to be a trophy wife? So where are you gonna find this guy?"

"Oh, I don't know," she said, feeling her cheeks grow warm.

"Well, I guess you can become a cheerleader or a dancer for a major sports team—or is that too much work for you? How about you do a music video? I mean, really, you have your pick of athletes and entertainers. Careful though—they might not marry you just for giving it up."

She knew he was now trying to be supportive and pretend he wasn't judging her, but she was furious again.

"Well, what about you?" she asked, unable to quench the violence in her voice, defenses still raised.

Bluto shrugged. "If my dad has his way, I'll be joining the military right after high school. I don't know—I could probably play football I guess, 'cause of my size. And no, I won't marry you if I do."

He smiled at her.

She decided to smile back.

Then a heavy rustle alarmed them, putting them on guard, and they both held whatever they had in their hands like weapons.

When the disturbance turned out to be a possum, they both burst into nervous laughter.

HOGWASH

How many hours? How the hell many more hours
could they possibly have? Even if they had done
circles before, surely they should be nearly out by now.

Ralph wondered why Mr. Huntsman hadn't allowed
watches—it was driving him crazy not knowing the time.

He had never been outdoor-friendly, had never been
on a hike or camping in his life, although he had once
'camped' on the lawn with some friends when he was
much younger.

He spent his time outside of school on the internet—
checking out porn, minor gambling. It seemed his parents
hadn't quite caught on to the latter yet, since they hadn't
confronted him about it—or else they didn't care.

When his parents finally caught on to his porn
purchases, his dad told his mom he would handle it, and,
once they were alone in the bedroom that now

embarrassed him—a car for a bed, the midnight sky on his walls—with a small conspiratorial smile, his dad told him that he understood. It was like he didn't even care Ralph had "borrowed" his credit card.

His dad must've figured it was a good time to teach him about the birds and the bees anyway—as if he hadn't seen what grown-ups do in full detail already. The 'why' didn't matter to him, he only longed to see what it felt like.

With a satisfied look on his face, his dad left his room, thinking he had solved the problem, no doubt, that he had talked some sense into him. He had even told him that if he was tempted to see new things to just let him know and they would work it out.

Yeah, right.

Still, no harm, no foul—his father practically winked at him in silent consent.

Now, his parents were perhaps too distracted to bother reprimanding him about the smaller offenses.

They had been fighting a lot recently, and his dad was now missing a lot in the evenings. His dad used to have time for storytelling sessions with him and his sister, Amy, where they would each come up with some fanciful, outrageous tale, but now, his dad barely existed, and his mom, quiet as ever.

He wondered if his mom and dad still did it, then had a hard time imagining they would. They didn't seem the type—his dad, an adult version of him with red hair and blue eyes and glasses, who didn't look like he would have a clue where to put things, his mom...blech. He couldn't imagine his mom like that, all spread open. A mousy-looking woman with brown hair always kept in a ponytail, she just didn't look like she would allow it.

When Ralph heard shouting through muffled doors, he further blocked out the noise with headphones and porn; online couples seemed happy.

The internet also helped him understand what was happening to his body. Plus, he got to see different things that worked on girls. He didn't want to be a complete loser and clueless when his first time came; didn't want anyone laughing at him. He wanted to make sure the girl—whoever she ended up being—felt good and cried out like the internet girls.

He definitely knew who he wanted his first time to be with, though: Jenny Baldwin.

A few guys liked Jenny and thought she was cute, but not as many as those who were after Miranda Fleming. Miranda was beyond cute—she was hot: tanned skin, blue eyes, wavy, long brown hair, dimples, straight, white teeth. Miranda looked like she could be a lingerie model; most guys probably masturbated thinking about her.

But Jenny was smart—although not in any obnoxious kind of way. She scored well, but didn't show off, raising her hand at every opportunity. She paid attention in class, and looked like she understood all the lessons.

Sometimes she would wear her dirty blond hair down, sometimes pulled back in a braid.

Her eyes were a funny kind of color; in fact, Huntsman's eyes had been similar—a kind of light brown with green in it. Hazel-green—although sometimes they just looked brown, sometimes just green, but most times they looked somewhere in between.

Jenny was always ready with a smile, too, but wasn't flirty or trying to be everybody's friend, and she definitely didn't look like she gave it away.

She just had a way about her that was sure—like she didn't care whether someone thought she should wear her hair down and styled or not, whether she should wear sexier clothes, like short skirts. She wore jeans and T-shirts and other regular clothes, didn't make it so her breasts or butt cheeks were on display so you thought about them at night—about what it would be like to put a hand up her leg.

Ralph hoped others didn't think about her like he did —he couldn't help it. But it didn't start off this way.

At first he imagined the two of them talking, walking to classes together—her, a casual side braid over her shoulder coming to rest on some nondescript T-shirt or blouse, an irreverent pair of shorts or jeans. She didn't even wear earrings—but she didn't need them.

It was her damned smile that kept him wanting more.

She smiled at pretty much anyone who made eye

contact with her, but when she smiled at him it was like she really saw him, yet still had something to smile about. She just looked so welcoming and, well, forgiving. So open.

Soon his fantasies of her started going beyond school to light, casual dating. He would take her to a movie, his dad letting him drive the few blocks to the movie theatre despite just having a learner's permit. She would turn into his chest when something scared her, and when it was all over, they would kiss on the lips.

There was a time when his fantasy would stop there—at them promising to see each other again.

When he finally started fantasizing about them doing it, it was always gentle—not like the aggressive workout people seemed to get in the internet video clips.

He would slowly seduce her, get her to take off her clothes, and see what her breasts looked like, feel her skin and see if it was soft.

Jenny had a hardy look—like she could go through the whole act without breaking a sweat. She played sports—rugby, and volleyball—and was tall like Miranda but not as skinny. Although she looked powerful, she still managed to look like a girl.

When he felt up her leg he would discover shapely, strong legs that were indeed soft. He would touch every part of her: kiss her cheeks, her lips, her neck. Run his lips over her arms. He would take his time—not like those guys in the porn. He would kiss her breasts, her nipples, down her abdomen. He would lick her and touch her until she was begging for more. And then, filled with love and yearning they would make love, and she would tell him she loved him when it was over.

He even imagined asking her to be his wife someday. She just seemed the right type—she wasn't all quiet and mousy like his mom, whom he loved, but he couldn't imagine having a wife who didn't talk much or never seemed to have any real opinions about things.

Jenny was a real person—confident, sunny, smart and beautiful—at least to him. He wouldn't care if she couldn't cook, as long as that smile of hers greeted him when he came home from work. Plus, she looked strong and healthy enough to bear him sturdy sons. He didn't care what they looked like—whether they took after him or her—as long as she was their mother and his adoring wife.

She didn't even need to have a glamorous job—he would do whatever he had to make sure she had everything she needed and wanted.

Ralph smiled to himself.

He wondered if she could see in his eyes when she looked at him and smiled how much he loved her. He kind of hoped she did; if she knew, maybe he had a chance.

Ralph shook his head, still grinning to himself. His friends would surely laugh at him if they knew any of his thoughts.

He figured David might too, although he realized he had never seen David laugh or even smile. He had never seen anything on David's face but that same stony expression, in fact; almost as if he wasn't there. Like his skin and body functioned without a spirit.

It worried him—the emptiness of his eyes, the lack of expression.

"What are you looking at?" David asked suddenly, reminding him that someone was behind the mask after all.

"Just wondering about you is all," Ralph said. "I know why I'm here, and so do you, but I don't really know anything about you. You said you're here for petty theft. Is that it? It's just us now."

David looked away, his stride still confident and fearless.

Ralph decided to try again. "You got any brothers or sisters?"

"Just me," David replied to his relief.

"You're lucky," Ralph joked. "I have an annoying sister. I miss her though. And I know she'll be glad to see me when I get back. To tell you the truth, I kinda like that she's always in my face and in my business; she's the only one who thinks the world of me, I think—she looks up to me. Although I have no idea why." Ralph smiled, hoping his light, joking tone would bring more out of his inscrutable companion.

Ralph did indeed have an idea why his sister looked up to him: he did well in school—one of the reasons he figured his parents didn't go hard on him for his transgressions—and he was good at video games. Amy would sit and watch with interest, cheering him on through first-person shooters, RPGs. To her, he was probably good at everything.

Although she got on his nerves, Ralph looked forward to seeing her when he got home.

She looked a lot like him—red hair and freckles included—but had brown eyes like their mom. She also wore glasses—although hers were a bit thicker than his.

"Anyway, I think I screwed all that up with my latest."

The first time he had started a fire, it was because he was bored. No one had gotten hurt in that one—it was an old abandoned building.

This time, he had come so close to killing people in the last place he torched. The family managed to get out in time, but he remembered, as he peeked from the bushes, firemen bringing out a little girl that looked a bit like his sister—all pale-skinned and sort of pug nosed—screaming about their pet dog. He thought about his sister then, and was horrified at the thought of anything like that happening to her.

His footsteps were found on the site, and the investigators managed to track him down where, upon searching, they found his stash of matches and lighters, and even flint rocks. They also found his drawings with people, places, and animals ablaze; he couldn't look more guilty.

"I just love fires. I love watching them, feeling the heat. It's magical the way they erase everything. Everything twists and cracks just because the flames are around—a real power you can watch. So fuckin' hot—no pun intended. It's the ultimate feeling."

He had never seen his father so angry the night they discovered he was a suspect in the arson, had never seen his face so red, heard his voice so loud—at least directed at him. And his mom had looked so severely disappointed, he felt like he would never regain her respect. He felt disowned in that moment—in the disappointment in her eyes.

The worst part of all was the way his sister looked at him afterward, like he was no longer her hero. To see the respect vanish from her eyes, to hear her answer him in the days following with a simple yes or no, as if he was no longer worth actual discourse with, for her to stop trying to tell him about her day, answering "fine" or "okay" once Ralph finally started prodding her about what went on in her own young life, broke his heart.

Amy barely even looked at him when he talked to her. Whatever was in her hand was more interesting—pulling on Raggedy Ann's hair, flipping pages of a book.

Feeling like he had lost love and respect from his

family was punishment enough; he was done setting fires. And if successfully completing the camp was all they needed to forgive him, if it proved to them he was still worthy of respect, honor, and dignity, then so be it; he was still getting off easy as far as he was concerned.

"I like seeing things burn, and I don't think this wilderness retreat will change that, but it'll make my family feel better about me. They'll think I'm willing to work with them and on my issues, and that's fine with me; I caused trouble, so I work on being troubled—that's just how things work. Besides, I'll admit—I'm a bit jealous of my sister now. She admired me so much, emulated me so much, and now, she's becoming me, but a better version of me. Under the pressure of the trail I blazed, she's scoring better and more consistently in school than I did. She's on her way to going to a more prestigious school, preparing to skip sixth grade, and you know what? My mom always wanted a girl—I just happened to come first. Amy's her little dream, and I'm kind of incidental."

He paused. "I mean, I know my parents love me, it's just that—sometimes I wish parents would treat their boys like they treat their girls. They kind of just leave us alone to help us 'become a man' and everything, but how do we keep our ability to nurture our own women and children if they stop nurturing us? I feel like I'm burning up with so much I want to share with them, and all they do is pat me on the head."

Still, Ralph felt grateful for having generally understanding—if clueless—parents. They had been so ridiculous searching him before his trip to the airport, and one final time there, trying to make sure he had no matches or a lighter, or any other kind of fire starter.

Ralph thought it was the funniest thing—there they were, sending him off into a forest with a plethora of wood and dry leaves. As if he couldn't knock two of the right rocks together.

Plus, there was one thing right in front of their eyes—and his—they had missed that could easily concentrate the sun's heat: his glasses.

But his parents both had the dumb-smart thing going on; they always missed what was right in front of them.

Ralph couldn't tell if David had heard a word he had said.

He decided to give it one more shot: "When did your parents have enough of you?"

David looked at him in a way that made him think his patience was running out. "Okay, you want to know what I'm about so you can feel better about your decision, fine. Here's a bit about me: like I said, I'm an only child and my parents are real tiger parents, if you know what I mean. They believe in corporal punishment. I suffered countless beatings at their hands to do better, be smarter. They said I was a waste of time, they wished they never had me, they want to give me up for adoption—things like that. They thought I was an embarrassment, brought shame on them because I was so dumb. I'm just an average kid—I get Bs and Cs—but that's nowhere near good enough for them. Not even an A- would work. They would joke between them, wondering aloud if I was switched at birth because no son of theirs could be such a dumb-ass. So I lashed out sometimes. I became really good at one thing—although I knew for sure they wouldn't approve of it: I became a petty thief. Not that I needed the money, but I liked pulling the wool over someone's eyes, outsmarting someone in a moment— people of all ages, races, colors, creeds. Most people don't even bother to suspect me, which I get a kick out of. They inevitably look around and their eyes settle on someone darker-skinned in suspicion. I like to work around blacks if I can."

David snickered. "People are so racist, and that cracks me up even more—watching some guy having to defend himself over nothing. Anyway, it became kind of a social experiment for me: to see how people would react when they realized they'd been pick-pocketed or thought they'd just lost some item. To see who they looked around at to suspect. To see how many would get bold and aggressive enough in their accusations and conclusions. I saw this one lady start outright hitting this poor guy with her purse telling him to give her phone back. Most people like that are pretenders anyway—acting like they don't see race or color, but the minute they're in a situation, their real feelings about groups come out.

"For me—everyone expects me to do well in school, to be some kind of super-achiever. To excel in math, but definitely not English. People actually say things like 'your English is so good!' or call me a Chinaman—and I'm an American! Born and raised here, speaking English all my life. I know a bit of Cantonese because my parents speak it at home, but even they hide who they are outside of it. They try to speak perfect English, which is fine—I don't blame them since they both live here permanently, but some other stuff they pull..." David shook his head. "They have no intention of letting me be an average American, yet they also want me to be a perfect Chinese boy— although if we'd been in China, that probably wouldn't change.

"One thing I've noticed here is that no one really wants you to be yourself. The more like 'the norm,' you can be the better. Whether you have to start wearing blue contacts, flat-ironing naturally curly hair, taking drugs, over-sexualizing yourself, speaking a certain way, or conforming to some stereotype. Gay people just can't be gay without persecution, atheists can't be atheists, Arabs can't be individuals, educated minorities have to be sellouts, low-class trailer folks have to be white trash. This place is not just a breeding ground for identity crises, it's a factory."

Ralph decided to ask no more questions as they walked on.

———

Daytime was bewitching.

Ralph felt much safer than he probably should have, simply because visibility had increased. Shadows no longer teased, sounds behind bushes were made insignificant by light, and everything was beautiful again.

Ralph noticed David checking Mr. Huntsman's GPS.

"So we're on the right path?" Ralph asked. "Out of here in no time?"

David looked at him in almost an accusatory way. "Yes," he said.

Ralph looked around at the trees, thankful the day looked like it would be bright.

He couldn't imagine losing his glasses in a place like this; it made him regret not pressing his parents for contacts. But the truth was, he liked his glasses. They made him feel a step away from everyone else, like he was watching safely from behind a mirror.

Ralph looked around and started taking pleasure in the beauty of the forest—the saturated green of mosses enveloping parts of trees, the curious twittering birds, the shade of the morning sky.

Natural beauty surrounded him in a way he had never

seen, so he easily noticed something out of place an hour later—a piece of iron perhaps, just sticking out of the ground.

He thought it oddly slanted at the tip, as if someone had cut it in an angle. He wondered what had been there.

David's attention seemed deflected as he went off to the left to inspect berries on a bush.

Ralph kept walking a few paces ahead, then suddenly realized he was stuck, then sinking. He started resisting the oddity happening at his feet, but it only seemed to get him more stuck.

"David, help me!" he shouted, wondering why he even needed to shout, why whatever David had found in the berry bush was so enthralling. "David!"

"I'm coming. Hold on, and calm down." David took off his backpack then knelt as he opened it up. "Don't panic, just stay still—you'll float. You'll be just fine."

Fine? He was going to drown to death in this heavy, wet dirt!

"It's probably not deep enough to drown you," David said, "but then again, you are kind of short." And then he giggled. Giggled! Ralph couldn't believe it.

"You think this is funny?"

"Well, sort of," David said, grinning. "Now just lay backwards. You've taken Physics, right? Wider area, less pressure. You'll spread your weight out and stop sinking; in fact, act like you're doing a backstroke as you lay back toward the edge. If you can kick your legs slowly it'll help loosen the dirt around you."

Then he pulled out a rope.

The guy was slick—Ralph hadn't even seen the rope in Huntsman's bag.

"Here, grab this."

Ralph reached up to grab the rope, closed his eyes, then held on for dear life, opening them only when he felt the firm ground scrape along his back.

The first thing David said was: "Well, the good news is, this means there's water nearby."

Ralph sat panting, trying to ignore the icky feeling of his clothes clinging to his skin.

He looked around at the forest. "Thought you'd have known that already. Don't you have the map and all that?"

Ralph felt a bitterness growing in him at his partner's indifference.

"Yeah, I know which general direction to go—I never said I knew where every spring of water or den of animals waiting to be our dinner were. I never said I knew where..."

"Okay, fine. Just...I'm pretty sure it would be marked on that map where water is."

"Fine, I'll take a look if it makes you feel better."

"Not sure it will, because I don't think you know which way's up by now." And more than that, Ralph suspected—however irrationally—that David had something to do with him encountering the quicksand. It was a gnawing feeling, something about the way David happened to wander away from it at just the right time, the way that metal rod was cut, as if a sign such as 'Be careful —quicksand ahead' could have once topped it. Something about the way he had so many useful things on him he wouldn't let Ralph get a look at.

Maybe David thought it was funny. Maybe he just wanted to mess with his head for kicks.

Ralph knew he might have just been paranoid, still shaken from his mishap, but maybe, just maybe David wanted him out of the picture so he could take the stuff in his bag as well—he was a petty thief after all.

THIRTEEN

PIGGYBACKING

Things Bluto wished he had: his iPod; he had tired of hearing Narine talk quickly. She didn't really have much to say, and all of a sudden, she was treating him like some kind of best friend—a girl best friend. Why the hell did she think he would give a fuck about what colors she looked best in? The latest thing she bought from MAC? He would even settle for a black and white TV with shows from the seventies; anything to distract from the yapping airhead next to him. And he would definitely rather eat dog food than listen to her say one more thing about the latest celeb news, reality TV crap, or fashion lines.

At this point, what he really wished he had was a muzzle so he could shut her ass up.

———

Things Narine wished she had: her cell phone most of all. She suffered from cell phone withdrawal tremendously—never imagined how dependent she had been on it. Just about everything she needed was on there. Anywhere she went, as long as she had reception, she would have everything at her fingertips.

She didn't know what she would spend more time doing if she had it right now: playing games, or listening to music.

Too bad she was stuck with this oaf who didn't know anything.

"No!" she had found herself screaming when caught with her cell, like her first born was being taken away. She had hated Jake Huntsman and his stupid rules about everything.

Another thing she wished she had right now: Jake Huntsman and his knowledge and direction.

———

For Narine, daylight ushered away some fears while bringing new ones—starving among them if they didn't get out of here soon.

"These stupid bars are totally ruining my diet," she said.

"Fuck, it's been, what, two days? Besides, you look

great—stop complaining. Even with your hair all fucked up like that."

Narine's hand immediately went to her hair to find the problem, and Bluto laughed.

"Yeah, but you like it," she said. "You're making fun now, but all you guys are the same. You'd prefer we look good than anything else. I'm only slipping a little because we're out here in this hellhole, and you're only here with me because you think I'm pretty."

"I won't deny that, but don't act like you're not with me for what I can do for you based off of my strength and power. You and me—this is how men and women are supposed to be."

Then he looked at her, his expression full of meaning, but turned his head forward, not saying anything else for the next few minutes.

This time, it wasn't the silence that made Narine feel uncomfortable—something else was in the air.

For one, Bluto seemed to be walking closer to her than ever.

So far, the severity of their situation had distracted from her false, silent promise to him, but now that they had been hiking without incident for a while, he must've felt safe enough to imply they had time to fool around.

She didn't feel so safe, however—she was terrified. Here she was, ninety-eight pounds, five feet four inches, and there he was—well over two hundred pounds, and six feet tall.

What was she thinking to go off with a guy like him? Thinking she would be protected?

His eyes concerned her most—the way he looked at her now, not bothering to hide his desire. He became more obvious in his flirting, playing more suggestive word games.

He kept sneaking a peek at her boobs, looking longingly at her lips.

She kept dodging, but knew this was a game she was sure to lose if he decided to turn the tables. She was running out of time.

She didn't know how much longer she had, but maybe it wasn't long before Bluto had enough of her stalling and took what he wanted.

If anything, he would at least try to kiss her soon, and she knew exactly what that meant. Kisses were only precursors, and if she went with it and let him get that close, she would be doomed; the rest wouldn't be too far behind.

If he decided he had waited long enough, there was no one around to help her, to hear her cries. He could easily take her down if he wanted to, against a tree.

Fear overwhelmed her and she fought to keep it under control. She couldn't let him smell it—she had to take charge of the situation. Emitting fear sometimes activated the attack instinct in other animals; she knew that—like with dogs.

She just needed to keep stalling, somehow; she would have an easier time getting away from him once they got out of the forest and there were people around.

She took a few deep breaths.

He was waiting for her reply—any reply to his latest innuendo.

"If only there was some creek or spring or something around," she said. "I feel so dirty." *Be careful Narine, you might excite him more.* "Anyway, it shouldn't be long before we get back," she said. "We're all sweaty and yucky, and you know how I like to look and smell clean and pretty..."

Lame, lame, lame. Why didn't you just tell him you were on your period?

Then Bluto smiled at her—an odd smile she couldn't quite interpret.

"I know what you're thinking," he said. "And I wouldn't do that to you—to anyone, believe it or not. Like I told you, I have a sister, and I know to some people that means nothing, but it means something to me. She's an adorable, nine-year-old towhead, and I help protect her by treating women with respect. I've never hit a woman or anything like that—can't imagine picking on someone that way."

"But you're a brute, Bluto—a bully, plain and simple."

"Yeah, but *that's* not the same thing."

Narine didn't care to hide her relief, and let out a heavy breath. "Well, I'm glad to hear it." Then, curiosity got the better of her. "What is it you're protecting your sister from? You keep talking about her like she's in some kind of imminent danger."

And then, just like that, Bluto was in another world. His eyes sort of glazed, then his mouth tightened before spilling his story out. "I caught my dad about to...hurt her. He had his dick out and she was asleep and I guess he was about to wake her. I lost it—I just saw red and attacked him. I don't even remember what I did—I just know he was unconscious by the time I realized I had kicked the shit out of him. I thought he was dead at first, but then I checked to see if he was breathing and he still was. His face was busted, several different colors—blue, red and black. And Cindy was just screaming and screaming and crying. She had no idea what was about to happen, and why dad was now on the floor—at least I hope she didn't. I had to explain I just saved her from getting hurt from him, and I couldn't tell her how. There's no way I could introduce her to filth like that."

"So it's not some random kid at school you sent to the hospital—it was your dad," Narine said in wonder.

"He was plastered—claims I attacked him while he was tucking her in." Bluto hung his head. "I never thought I'd have it in me to do that to him. But of course, I didn't know he had *that* in him either. Anyway, dad's in the hospital, I'm here, Cindy's in foster care—somewhat safe for now. Even if dad got out before I get back, they won't just hand her to him; our place got inspected, and they didn't exactly find it up to snuff. I just have to make sure they don't hand her back to him ever; I'm making plans to get her in a good home."

"Your dad sure had it coming," Narine said, meaning every word.

Bluto looked grateful. "I'm glad you see it that way."

———

THINGS HAD BEEN GOING SO SMOOTHLY between her and Bluto despite not seeing signs of civilization ahead, that it took them both a moment to acknowledge the sudden, odd grunt in the air, and the violent rustling in the bushes.

Narine realized at what seemed like the same moment Bluto did, that the animal she had begun doubting existed was near.

Then she heard a horrible squeal, followed by more grunting and bushes rustling at the rapid progress the animal was making through the forest, the snapping branches and pounding of forest floor.

Neither of them waited to see what the creature looked like to confirm their suspicions.

They both started running in the direction they figured was away from the animal, knowing the creature had them in their sight, forgetting what the strange ex-military figure had said about the impossibility of outrunning a wild pig as they shed their heavy backpacks.

While running, Narine realized that Bluto couldn't protect her, that even if they were cornered, he would probably put her in front of him so the pig could get at her first. That the only reason he had been sniffing around her was because of their unspoken deal.

"Ever heard that joke about outrunning the bear?" Bluto said suddenly, confusing her momentarily, and she didn't have time to think about it as she felt his massive hand crash against her side so that she lost traction, her balance, and was suddenly out of the race.

"I just have to outrun you!" she heard him say as he sprinted on, and she remembered the joke after all:

Why are you putting on running shoes? You can't outrun a bear! One hiker said to the other as they encountered a grizzly.

I don't have to outrun the bear—I just have to outrun you!

But Bluto hadn't just shoved her down so that she became a sort of speed bump halting the animal's progress one way or another, she didn't just fall down on the path. The way he had pushed her threw her so off balance, and was so violent, that her body kept rolling and slid down the nearby embankment. Soon she was tumbling, hitting everything on her way down—bouncing on rocks, getting smacked in the face, the ass, by branches and bushes.

There went her expensive veneers, she was sure. She would be lucky if she even had all her teeth after this. And forget about carefully tamed hair; she would probably never get the tangles and brambles out.

There went her perfectly smooth, untarnished skin, as she felt her skin tear, cuts open, bruises born. There was no way she could be pretty ever again if she even managed to survive her fall.

———

BLUTO THOUGHT for sure he had improved his chances—surely the pig would stop to eat Narine, giving him all the time he needed to get up a tree.

He had heard Narine screaming, but her voice sounded funny, and started fading fast. He couldn't look back, couldn't spare that split second glance to see what was up—he might have run into a tree, or tripped over a rock, costing him precious seconds. He had to focus.

He had no doubt, however, that she had gone down.

But then he realized footsteps still pounded the ground behind him, catching up fast.

Could it be his plan hadn't worked?

Now he actually hoped it was Narine behind him, but

it was only wishful thinking—he heard the animalistic breathing, the odd snorting and chomping.

He soon spotted a viable tree and tried to scale it.

He jumped, arms reaching for a branch, then tried to climb up the trunk, feeling like a drunk monkey. The trunk laughed at him, so he turned back to the branch just there—right out of reach of his hands. He jumped and jumped, and realized he wasn't going to pull himself up on it—even after he managed to grab it with his hands—he just didn't have the strength to pull himself up onto the safety of the branch, to even get his legs up, and hang onto it like a sloth, despite his adrenalin.

He felt a sharp pain in his back as the pig's tusks reached him, and knew it was too late as he felt his skin stabbed over and over and over again.

His final thoughts were of his sister, Cindy, and briefly, his dad, as he hoped to God his dad perished in the hospital.

FOURTEEN

PIG IN A POKE

Things Ralph wished he had: the company of his dog Spotty, an English bull terrier. He wished for anything familiar right about now, and fire wouldn't be enough; he needed something at about 98.6 degrees, or whatever body temperature it was that dogs had. With Spotty would come affection, play, and challenges, all bundled into one adorable package. Plus a line of defense —but that would mean Spotty would be in danger out here.

Still, his dog would handle the outdoors so much better than he had, would help his attitude about everything. Spotty would probably have a blast out here, all wild and free. He wouldn't be afraid of some stupid pig; in fact, he would probably have a better chance of surviving a pig ambush than Ralph would.

What Ralph really wished he had right now was a lot

less time out here in the wilderness with a stranger who didn't give a shit about him.

"I'm starting to get hungry," Ralph said.

Then he heard a familiar, soft sound and his heart surged.

David also paused to listen. "Water," David said with what sounded like relief, and they hurried in its direction.

They saw what looked like a clearing through open trees with rocks—smooth flat ones, gnarly ones.

"Ugh! What the hell is that smell?" Ralph asked as they neared the hot springs.

"Well, hot springs are known to be a bit sulphuric—like rotten eggs."

"No way that's all the springs."

Ralph followed a humming sound he soon realized was a buzzing that turned out to be tons of flies around a horribly mangled dead body.

"Well, that kind of solves one of our problems," David said, "especially since you're good at making fires."

Ralph's blood froze. "What are you talking about?" he asked, ignoring the dread gathering in his stomach.

"You're hungry, aren't you? Would you really turn away what could be a good meal?"

Ralph turned and vomited.

When it felt like he had no more left in him to bring up, he turned to David, who had apparently found his bodily reaction immensely funny. The impassive face, that had only cracked a smile once at the quicksand, was now transformed in laughter, as if its owner had been given laughing gas.

"How can you do that?" Ralph asked. "How can you stand there and laugh when this body here..." Ralph felt himself about to retch again. He tried holding it back, knowing it would become painful if he were sent into a fit again as his stomach felt completely empty now.

"You should've seen your face," David said, still grinning widely, black eyes glittering. "But you're right—it's not exactly fresh meat. Probably not too healthy to consume even if we were to scorch it some."

Then David looked at him in a way that made Ralph wonder if he was waiting for him to lose it again. But something about the look wasn't right—the look of anticipation didn't quite match the look of waiting to be amused. David's eyes had gone sort of beady and animal-like.

"Right," was all Ralph could think of to say, no longer sure David had been kidding.

David tilted his head, and looked at him as if sizing him up. He had already done that before—had already pointed out how small Ralph was for his age, how weak he seemed overall.

"You probably can't see shit from squirrel without those glasses, huh?" he had asked earlier.

Don't sleep tonight, a small voice told Ralph from within. *Do not sleep around this guy again.*

Ralph suddenly realized he needed to protect himself from more than just a monster pig. He switched gears, now doubting everything the guy next to him had told him. Had he really been just a petty thief? Did he really do poorly in school? Was he really an only child?

Ralph also realized he needed to get a weapon somehow, some way. He needed to be able to defend himself should the chance come up, because this guy was not his friend.

Holding his nose, Ralph walked boldly over to the body and used his foot to check the man's pants but came up empty.

He remembered seeing a bag at the edge of the hot spring and headed back there.

He looked around before inspecting the contents, and triumph flooded through him when his hand connected with a gun.

He held on to the weapon, inspecting it, and when David's slow walk finally brought him to the spring, his face again reflected something that seemed genuine—an expression almost like respect, like he was seeing him in a new light.

"Don't even think about it," Ralph said to David before he could say anything. "This one's staying with me."

Ralph wasn't quite sure he knew how to use the weapon, but if it could keep at least one animal at bay, it had already proven useful.

———

DAVID'S PARENTS threatened to send him to China to live with his grandma and uncle—folks they thought could handle him better than they could.

He did well in school as demanded, and had a high IQ like his mom, but they'd caught him in too many lies, and none of them wanted a problem child—it interrupted their American dream.

But they could forget forcing him to go to China—he was a born-and-bred American, and even if they had bought his ticket, then saw him through to airport security, he would have escaped. He wasn't sure where he would have gone, but there was no way he would leave his country.

He could figure out lodgings easily on his own— pickpocket hotel funds for example—finding somewhere to sleep and food would be no problem.

What David really wanted was his mom at the continental chess tournament in two months, to show her he was champ, then challenge her to a game she wouldn't be able to beat him at again. And the only way he was allowed to continue his tournaments was to do this wilderness retreat.

Sure, he could have easily faked parental consent, but he didn't want to put his title at risk; he wanted to be a legal entrant and champion.

Chess wasn't a big deal to them, but they liked when he won things; it made them proud, and he liked making them proud. They probably worried about him being defective, and he needed them to see his worth.

David had been allowed to bring along his chess set for this trip, the camp leader considering it for a moment, then probably figuring he couldn't use it against anyone. Hell, he probably even expected him to bring something nerdy along.

David had had several sessions with unlikely chess masters in preparation for his tournament and beating his mother at the game at last—amongst them: a mid-thirties Iraq war vet, an old woman in a retirement home, and a homeless man with salt and pepper dreadlocks. He had planned to work on his strategy on this wilderness journey, but hadn't yet gotten a chance to do so since embarking on it.

Instead, a different game emerged, one far more interesting, and combining two of his favorite past-times. He had succumbed to the immediate parental threat to his chess goals by agreeing to do this camp, but now he was more than glad he had agreed to it—he couldn't have created a more stimulating environment.

Here, he could play the type of game that got him to this retreat in the first place, in a different arena.

Harassing weaklings online thrilled him, and proved over and over what his father always said—the weak don't deserve to live. Nature's goal was always to weed them out and let the strongest of the species survive—or at least, those most fit for it at the time, whatever that entailed.

David's first victim had been a girl at school, some slut sleeping with the high school basketball coach.

David managed to figure out their favorite spots to have sex, and in one of them, he planted a camera. He caught her not only giving the coach a blow-job, ending with him splattering all over her face, but also a few minutes of actual sex.

It was one of his personal favorite videos.

He had uploaded it to YouTube using his false email account linked to it, and quietly tipped off a few people in school about it.

He didn't even have to say anything to the girl on the sly in person—everyone else said everything for him. She probably hadn't known there were so many ways to call someone a whore, and she could not overcome her mortification of having performed on the coach.

As for the coach, he got fired immediately, charged with statutory rape, lost his wife, his kids, his reputation.

That's where David liked to get people—their reputation—the thing people spent so many years to build that was so easy to come crumbling down. Like buildings.

His companion, Ralph, probably understood that well, having destroyed structures that had taken months upon months, or even years to build in one night.

David had gotten a two-for-one deal with the coach and the slutty junior high girl—after a rather short campaign playing her fictitious sympathetic online friend, she jumped from the roof of a fourteen-story building, and the coach eventually hanged himself.

David didn't quite understand people hanging themselves—it seemed potentially an unnecessarily slow, painful way to go. He had always wondered—what if you changed your mind in one of those last seconds? What if a broken neck didn't kill you right away? What about the horrible bloated purple mess you would leave behind? But part of him thought there was some strength in it.

Weak was sleeping pills, carbon monoxide; hanging took some kind of balls.

David had also preyed on an ugly, fat girl at school—an easy target. Investigators thought everyone was responsible for that one—her parents, some of the mean, pretty girls at school, TV commercials, society at large. He had played an online boyfriend in that case, and she had gone the way of slit wrists.

The kid who had actually gotten him caught was

pathetic too—insecure, felt rejected by society, and was probably sure his family would shun him once they found out he was gay. Like it was such a big deal these days.

It wasn't enough for David to get him in person, calling him names. David found him online, and posted comments underneath his comments, virtually stalking him. He managed to catch him spilling his guts to someone about his predicament and posted the confession to the web.

Unfortunately, the boy died with his computer screen up, and David didn't have enough time to swipe it and make any evidence leading to him disappear. He hadn't expected the boy to get so ballsy and blow his brains out with his dad's gun—and so soon; he had barely started in on him.

David could only shake his head when he heard the news. What a dumb-ass—he only proved correct everyone who had teased him; he couldn't survive in today's world, and again, he didn't blame the boy for taking himself out— it was the natural way of things.

It wasn't his fault his victims were so weak. If they didn't kill themselves when they did, they would have done it within ten years or so; one thing or another would have taken them over the edge. They did humanity a favor erasing themselves from the gene pool.

His father had looked so disappointed when he found out what he had done—the most feeling he had shown in a while. David was glad to see it. Part of him thought his dad would be proud even, but there was no trace of pride in the old, brown leather face. Even his white hair seemed to stick out in disapproval. How did his mom end up marrying such an old guy anyway?

Son, why would you do this? Why would you pick on your classmates like this?

David had wondered how his father knew there was more than one—why he had said 'classmates' when only the boy—Leroy, the drama queen—had been linked to him.

David fumbled his answer. *They are weak, wouldn't you say, father? That is not my fault.*

His father had struck him across the cheek and sent him to his room.

You are a monster, his dad said to him, a phrase that echoed in his head for days after. *And you are weak. You are no son of mine.*

Weak? How could one with such power be weak?

Despite his father's words, David detected a hint of fear. Could his own father be afraid of him? If he was, he didn't blame him.

David felt the beginnings of the same feelings that came to him when he located another potential victim.

The sense of power made a slow takeover of his body as he became aware that he could quite easily do away with his dad and get away with it.

The day he left for the camp, his mother saw him off

while his father was asleep in his car, engine on in the closed garage.

As he thought of his mother making the grisly discovery once he was already off on his wilderness adventure, he realized too late that his sense of power had to be controlled.

He wasn't sure how things would go once he got back, couldn't think about it. Maybe his mother would hold him dearer if his father had perished, but what if he hadn't? Would he suspect his son had knocked him out and set him up? Did worse consequences await him?

Luckily, this camp delighted him so far, entertained him, kept his mind off of it.

He was especially enjoying getting to know Ralph—the boy, like that sickly, pale girl who had run off and not come back, was a weakling. Ralph thought he had strength in fire, but David would show him otherwise.

His father always said: "luck is when preparation meets opportunity," and David had prepared for this camp in several ways, had researched the area long before getting into the van—learned which plants were okay to handle, which to stay away from. He knew about the animals they were likely to encounter.

Besides, he wasn't stupid; he didn't ace all his classes for nothing.

Plus, he had come into the camp with a skill—another type of luck: he happened to be faster on the draw than the other boneheads in the camp. Too preoccupied by the simple things, the obvious, they missed all the objects that seemed insignificant, but were more important than some serrated knife. Such a knife was indeed handy in a wilderness, but if they were really going to be pursued by a giant, rabid, man-eating pig, the knife was useless.

With Jake Huntsman's GPS unit, David knew where he was at all times. He knew where to go, how to get out of the wilderness whenever he wanted to—he just wasn't ready to leave the losers yet; he hadn't had this much fun in a while.

———

"Let me show you something," David said, indicating to Ralph to come closer.

David traced out a route on the map. "We go this way from here, and a service station is just there—a few hours at most."

"Well, let's do it!" Ralph exclaimed, his joy causing his voice to squeak a little.

"I don't know about you, but there's no way I'll make it all the way without eating something, anything, right now; I'd probably fall out before we get there. Someone robbed my backpack of food—I guess when I went to pee when we were on the campsite. I haven't eaten since then."

Ralph was about to protest, but realized he was being

selfish. Would it really hurt to get stalled by half an hour or so? They had lots of daylight ahead of them.

He realized his protest actually came from the idea of being alone in the wild while David went off to find food.

He expressed his fear to David, and David agreed to walk a bit further until they found a tree he could climb up if needed.

Ralph sat at the base of it, his ears sharply in tune to the noises around him in the quiet of David's absence.

When he heard a steady, deliberate gait crunching through the forest, he knew it was probably a person, but stood, prepared to scale the tree anyway.

David emerged with vegetation.

"I found us lunch," David said, smiling, dropping the pile of plants and mushrooms down. "We'll make soup or something—something like my mom makes at home. Or is that not good enough for you?"

"No, it's fine," Ralph said quickly, not wanting to offend him.

"Good. Why don't you get the fire started since that's your forte?"

Ralph smiled at him gratefully.

Then his stomach grumbled. He hadn't realized how famished he felt himself. He had munched on bar after bar through the initial hike, after rushing through the forest to find trees to settle in, and in the quiet boredom of their first night as they waited out the dark in trees. And definitely in the hours of walking since. He, too, had depleted his three-day supply of food.

————

THIS IS GOING to be too easy, David thought, watching Ralph, although Ralph had been a bit wary of the mushrooms at first.

"You sure those are okay?" he had asked.

"Don't these look familiar to you? Your mom probably buys them in the grocery store too—they just look a little different because they're in the wild—no one's prepared them for consumers yet, making them look pretty and clean. Look, I'll just throw them away if you're so scared—I'm not eating them by myself like some prisoner on the holidays. I just thought it would be cool if we could just have a sort of nice meal together; I'm trying to be social here. I even got these greens to spice it up a bit."

Sold. He could see it in Ralph's eyes; he had reeled him in—hook, line, and sinker. Guilt was a hell of a string to pull.

When Ralph dug into the mushrooms, David took his time pretending to get started, blowing it, as if it was still too hot for him.

"You sure are slow," Ralph said. "Thought you were starving?"

"I want to savor the moment more. What am I, some animal?"

Ralph giggled, almost contagiously excited about the meal in front of them, and probably the lie about them being a few hours away from safety.

Then David shifted, spilling his portion from the makeshift bowl.

"Shit," he said.

"You can have some of mine," Ralph offered, but David shook his head and let out a heavy breath.

"I'll go grab some more. Probably just eat them raw, I'm so hungry. Be right back."

He took off, but watched Ralph from the forest.

It wasn't long before David saw something different about his face—his eyes. He knew the effects of the mushroom could start as early as thirty minutes, but perhaps because Ralph was so small, or because he hungrily ate so many of the mushrooms, his change began a bit sooner.

David's plan kicked into gear. "Take a little nap," he said when he returned. "A break before the last push home. Give yourself some time to relax; we're safe now."

Ralph's agreeability and suggestibility had spiked. "All right then," he said, laying on the grass.

David chuckled and wrapped him in a blanket.

Ralph smiled like a baby. "Thanks, bud," he said, closing his eyes.

————

WHEN RALPH OPENED HIS EYES, he wasn't sure what had happened—his vision had blurred, and it looked like night again. He put his hand at his eyes and discovered his glasses gone.

He reached around himself trying to locate them, but his hands came up empty.

He threw the blanket off himself, and sat up, feeling around again. Then he stood, remembering he had been allowed to bring an extra pair.

He looked around and made out a grayish brown lump. His heart leapt, fear choking him.

"David?" he called out tentatively, his voice embarrassingly plaintive. Then relief flooded him as David replied.

"You're up! What's up?"

"Can you hand me my backpack?"

David brought the grayish brown lump he had questioned to him.

Ralph searched and searched as panic rose in him and he came up empty.

He tried to remain calm. Maybe he could get away with pretending to see more than he could. But how was he supposed to fool anyone? David would see through him like he saw through his thick bifocals.

David had probably taken them anyway. And now

David, the animals, the changes in terrain, the trees, rocks —everything was an enemy to him; anything could sneak up on him.

David's voice came as if from far away:

"While you were out I went exploring a bit, and guess what—I saw the pig up ahead by a group of rocks. Well, maybe not *the* pig, but a wild one nonetheless. It was pretty ugly—I think I might be turned off from eating bacon and shit now after looking at that thing."

"What did he look like?"

"Dark gray with hair all over, and he had these tusks— four of them, two coming up from the bottom, two coming out from the top. Boy, I wouldn't want to get caught between them."

"How come he didn't come after you?" Ralph paused and listened. "And it sounds like he's still not headed this way..."

"He's probably scared of us, Ralph."

The thought elated him. "Yeah, we can't be fucked with." Ralph grinned at his companion. "You're crazy, huh, David?" He felt oddly amused by his own honesty and in a great mood. "Did you mean to switch Joe and Bluto's bags yesterday?"

David ignored his questions. "Honestly, the hog was sleeping. I'm not even sure that's what that guy was talking about—I mean, it was big, but not as big as that guy made it seem. Plus, I don't think it can run as fast as he said, or get very far without collapsing. I mean, imagine a three-hundred-pound human chasing you through the forest—don't you think he'd get tired fast?"

"Yeah. Just a big ol' fat guy. Maybe he was just talking about the average pig. Anyway, we should probably get out of here; I think we've overstayed our welcome."

"You do realize the pig is toward the main path?"

"But we don't need to hang here longer than we need to—the shortest way from B to G is a straight line. I mean, A to B. And anyway, if you don't think that was the homicidal pig you saw, we can probably just take it out, right? We should probably kill it while it's sleeping. We could have meat for days!"

Ralph smiled, feeling like his smile extended beyond his face.

He didn't know what he was talking about—meat for days? They wouldn't be here that long; his mind was soggy. Still, everything made perfect sense—kill the sleeping pig, and they would be able to keep moving forward.

Damn, the forest was beautiful.

He barely heard David's next words:

"But you'd have to unload the gun on the pig, Ralph—we don't have the kind of weapon that could keep us safe while it thrashes around and dies slowly, yet still comes after us, angry. Are you willing to stand there and keep shooting at it?"

Ralph's body felt odd to him. He had snuck into his father's bar once, and tasted a couple of bottles there. Then he felt kind of woozy and unstable after. He couldn't even walk straight.

What he felt now was sort of similar.

Sometimes it felt like his head was falling to the side and he better catch it! Or else it would keep falling and roll right off down the side. And then everything he saw looked like a cartoon. Sparks flew with more life than usual—as if they were shrunken shooting stars. And the fire—it was sometimes like looking through a concave mirror, sometimes looking through a convex mirror.

David seemed to be smiling somehow although his mouth was a line. His eyes kept changing sizes—one big and warped, the other small, then vice versa, like they were in some kind of dance.

Ralph tried lifting his hand and eventually it cooperated. He lifted the other. Then he raised and lowered them in succession, as fast as he could, as if playing a piano.

It made him giggle.

"Ralph," David's voice sang to him.

Why David's voice doubled on itself like a piggybacking echo was beyond him. It sounded like it was coming through some sort of vacuum from above.

"I'm gonna need you to spread the fire—the pig's coming; let's block it out."

Ralph's heart thumped, sounding in his ear.

He squinted, as if that would make sense of the mess of colors and shapes.

"Fire, Ralph. Keep it out, just like you said! Make a wall all around; lighter fluid's near your feet."

Ralph worked frantically.

He found the nearby fluid where his weapon had been, and began to draw a line between him and the danger until he was surrounded in a safe circle. He hoped he hadn't accidentally left David out.

He lit the liquid, then watched the fire burst into a beautiful circle dancing around him.

Ralph thought about Jenny Baldwin, and committed to telling her how he felt about her as soon as he got back.

He felt warm and safe. And turned on.

The trees rippled and bled around him, the sparks exploding into fireworks.

He sat down to admire the view, immersed in his fiery castle. As the heat increased, his body tingled with heightened arousal and he felt himself growing hard. Then he heard a grunting sound just feet away and he rose to his feet. There, close enough to see, was the feral pig.

The beast was huge, its back almost six feet off the ground. It shook and bristled as it paced in front of the fiery wall.

Its head sloped forward as if to distance itself from the gnarled tusks that tore through its filthy, bloodstained face.

Covered in matted hair that collected the filth of the forest as camouflage, it seemed bigger than a rhino. It slapped its jaws together in frustration.

Ralph calmly took in the abomination, a sense of peace engulfing him.

He felt safe in the fire, even while the beast became more impatient as the fire rose, circling and shrieking outside of the glowing ring.

Ralph sat down again and smiled, knowing the beast would never get him.

FIFTEEN

BRINGING HOME THE BACON

T hings Joe wished he had: body lotion. Or face lotion or hand lotion or whatever—he didn't understand the difference anyway. Any kind of lotion—his skin felt so dry. He wished he could stop the bug bites, so he wished for bug spray as well; in fact, he didn't know which one he wanted more.

He figured he probably lost a big can of bug spray in the fight for that crazy knife with Bluto.

Each of them had been issued bug repellent in their bags, but Joe felt like it was no longer enough—like some of the bugs had gotten used to it and had no problem biting right through it.

"Aloe," Luz said, "if we can find aloe, that'll help."

He didn't question her and kept his eyes open for the prickly looking plant as she described it.

They didn't find any.

At some point they stopped noticing the bug bites on their arms.

"I hope they're not carrying anything—these mosquitoes, and whatever else has been eating us alive," Luz said. "The baby, you know? I want her to be healthy."

———

THINGS LUZ WISHED SHE HAD: a tub, a shower. Soap and water and a bucket. Anything like that; she had never felt so dirty in her life, never thought she could feel so gross, so nasty, so filthy. And those stupid baby wipes they had been issued didn't do anything.

She had heard hot springs were around, and wished out of everything in the world they could run into one now. She was almost tempted to go backwards for a bit, and find one they had left behind, but she knew that was just stupid. No doubt it would increase their time in danger in the forest, and their chances of being attacked.

She thought instead about how much closer a real bath and shower would be if they just kept going forward.

She tried not to panic about having not come across a view of the main roads even after making it through the night and some of the day.

Still, it was just afternoon. They would likely reach some sort of safety while the sun was still out, and she could last until then.

WHAT JOE KNEW they both wished they had: food.

They at least had some water left, but Luz had to be starving, and so was he. They had finished their bars, and had run into some blueberries, but knew they couldn't risk it; they didn't know which ones were poisonous yet.

It saddened Joe that Luz was having such a hard time. Her energy was waning, she was getting slower, weaker. He had been able to power through, but she was hungry for two.

Joe knew he had to do something.

He hated to do it, couldn't believe it had come to this, but he had to hunt down and kill one of the forest creatures.

A rabbit, maybe? They could start with that—he could be okay with that. It was just a matter of figuring out how to catch one. And didn't people eat frog legs? He had seen a couple of those creatures around. And then there was that yellow slug, but it just looked like something he shouldn't eat—even if it seemed easy enough to catch, and he had heard of people eating snails.

Still, he knew they had other options. Joe had heard snakes tasted like chicken, but he definitely wasn't sure he wanted to try his luck with those, even if no poisonous ones were around. A deer he couldn't do—a deer would be too much. What would they need with all that meat

anyway? It would only go to waste, at least to them—
something else would probably come along and finish the
carcass off. Besides, he knew he didn't have the heart to
capture and kill one, not after *Bambi*. No, a squirrel or
rabbit it was. Maybe even a wild turkey if they were lucky
—Mr. Huntsman had mentioned those too.

"I'm going to give it a shot, Luz," Joe said.

He looked at the trees around them and found one
that looked promising. "I'll put you up there," he said with
confidence. "I'll make it comfortable first." Joe gathered his
tent and a few extra clothes and climbed about fifteen feet
to the split in the tree that looked like a three-fingered
hand, and he built a small nest.

"Great, I'll fly up there," Luz said with a playful smile.
Joe carefully climbed down, and as he reached the last
branch, reached down to Luz. She grabbed his hand, and
was lifted smoothly up into the air until with the least of
effort, she was able to sit on the first branch. He climbed
ahead and repeated the process until she was placed in the
makeshift nest.

———

As Joe made his way into the forest, he imagined
himself a seasoned hunter. He crouched slightly as he
moved along and around the unpredictable forest floor.
His eyes darted here and there. He heard everything. He

moved deeper into the dark, canopied area where he was sure the prey animals would hide during the day. He moved swiftly, bounding through the terrain in near-silence.

He froze suddenly at the sound of what turned out to be a weasel. He barely shifted his feet when the weasel made him, and bolted out of sight.

He stood tall and took a deep breath. Maybe his bright yellow shirt didn't help his purposes.

He removed the shirt and tied it around his waist and stuffed moss around it. He even smeared some soil on his chest and face. He had seen this on TV, and it felt right in the moment.

He retook his hunter stance and continued on.

A rabbit was in sight, and most importantly, Joe had seen the log it kept returning to. He made his way above the hollow log, slowly sliding up a mature tree that had half-fallen.

Just a few feet above him now, the rabbit moved about its daily business. As it returned to the log, Joe felt his moment had come. In that moment, he realized he had not thought about this part, and had no way to catch or kill the little creature.

He dropped down like a bomb on the log, which crumbled under his fall.

He waited to hear a little rabbit cry or feel a bit of struggle.

After a moment, he picked himself up and sifted through the crushed moist log—nothing.

As he stood, about to cry out in frustration, he saw the beast.

Fear numbed him, and he did not move or even breathe.

Had the bear seen him?

It was plodding along, swinging its head back and forth aimlessly.

Joe blinked his eyes and the bear stopped.

I am supposed to act big, Joe remembered.

The bear looked at him, then rose to its hind legs and snorted violently. Turning toward him, it dropped down and let out a short roar.

Before the bear could charge, Joe stepped out into the open, covered in mud and all manner of grass and moss, and raised his arms to the sky, letting out a tremendous war cry.

The bear rose again, but did not react immediately. It seemed momentarily confused by the display.

Joe wondered what was supposed to happen next— would the bear wander off now? How long should he stand here like this?

A rustle at Joe's feet distracted him—the rabbit, half-crushed, but alive and twitching.

Joe glanced at the bear and moved one arm down

slowly to retrieve his dinner. As he tucked the rabbit in his waist band, the bear erupted into an earsplitting roar.

Joe had never heard anything so loud and intense, and the sound seemed to go on for over a minute.

He turned and began to run.

The bear battered the forest floor behind him as the chase began.

Joe flew through the forest, swinging over logs and leaping over rocks and patches of twisted branch, while the bear blasted through the forest obstacles.

Joe had to make a move.

He leapt for a high branch and caught it with one hand.

As he struggled to secure himself, the bear came barreling closer.

Joe finally pulled himself up, and the bear smashed into the tree, shaking Joe to his core.

Joe looked down, hoping the collision had somehow hurt the animal, but he saw it backing up steadily.

The second blow devastated the trunk of the tree, and it cracked and popped as it began to free fall.

Joe climbed up, then along the falling tree, hoping to be as far from the bear as possible when he landed.

He hit the ground hard, wind leaving his body, but the bear was still coming.

He again broke into a sprint, knowing he needed a safe

place, a stronger tree, and soon spotted one much larger, but harder to climb, lacking in lower limbs.

He headed for the tree, leaping to reach the lowest branch that could support him, swiftly finding himself secure.

He gasped for breath, momentarily putting the bear behind him.

Then a scratching thud grabbed his attention.

Bears can climb trees!

His legs dangling below him, Joe clenched the large branch above him and looked down.

The bear was coming.

He was too high up to jump—the ground below him rocky, and covered in boulders and dry logs.

The bear made its way closer with each passing moment, its claws ripping into the tree as it pulled itself up toward him.

For the first time, Joe believed he would die—probably knocked from the tree and eaten over the rocks below. The bear would probably even get his rabbit.

Suddenly Joe felt a sharp jab at his side as the bear's claws ripped through him.

Joe came back to life.

He kicked at the pawing beast, and even poked it in the face and eyes with a loose branch he managed to rip off the tree. Nothing seemed to do more than bother the large creature.

He decided to take one last action. He climbed higher, positioning himself above the bear. Then he tucked his arms before dropping straight down, feet first—his body rigid and tight, acting as a torpedo striking the bear with concentrated force. The impact twisted the animal's head as his feet met the animal's lower jaw.

The collision seemed to stop everything—the bear lost its grip and slipped off the tree, the two falling to the unforgiving earth below.

With Joe riding him down, wrapped around his head and neck, the bear fell flat on its back, and Joe bounced off, coming to rest against a group of decayed logs.

Joe realized he had been spared a rocky death by the bear's immense body absorbing most of the impact.

He heard the bear crying out pitifully and regained himself, heading toward the now obviously immobile animal.

The bear had probably broken its back, in addition to its other injuries.

Joe no longer saw anything wild about the animal, its resigned look almost human; in fact, it looked almost pleading for relief as its eyes met his.

Joe kept up the eye contact, trying to reassure the creature that he understood what it needed.

Joe checked for his rabbit, then searched for the largest rock he could find—one that would ensure finality.

"Oh my god, Joe—what the hell happened to you?"

Luz's eyes were large and filled with fright and worry as she climbed out of the tree.

Joe dumped the dead creature down.

"Catching that rabbit couldn't have caused that much trouble?" she asked.

Joe let out a breath.

"I killed a bear...or it got killed...No, I killed it."

Luz's mouth dropped. "You *what?*"

"Well, I surprised it, I guess, but it surprised me too—I sure wasn't expecting it. He was hunting too, I think. Next thing I knew, it came after me. Mr. Huntsman said not to ever run from one or else they'll come after you, but it didn't serve me no good *not* running because it came after me anyway. I made a bunch of noise and waved my hands, and I guess he thought I meant to step into the ring, because he loved it. Anyway, most importantly, I'm back, and we're going to be fine."

Luz's mouth still hung open, and she watched him incredulously. "You killed a bear?"

"I had to—he had me trapped, and I couldn't get away."

Joe didn't know if she was impressed or disappointed.

She definitely seemed stunned into silence. Then she

looked around, as if suspicious the bear's family would come upon them seeking revenge.

"Luz, don't be scared. If another one comes, we'll be eating bear next," he reassured her, sounding braver than he felt.

Luz slowly bent to her backpack, then retrieved the first aid kit. Her hands shook as she extracted a few items from it. "I can't believe you threw down with a bear—how far away did you go? I didn't even hear anything."

She stopped picking through the kit to look at him directly with what almost looked to him like disapproval in her eyes. "Do you have any idea how crazy that is? Not just anyone can kill a bear."

Joe shrugged. "I just pretended it was Bluto."

This cracked her up, and it made him grin back at her.

Then she looked down, her smile disappearing. She took stock of his injuries once more—particularly his right side where the bear had gotten through his flesh with teeth or claws—he couldn't remember.

"It's not as bad as it looks," he insisted.

"Yeah, well. It sure looks bad. And it's still bleeding."

She cleaned him up, disinfecting his wounds, then bandaged him in silence for the next few minutes.

He appreciated the quiet moments, the chance to watch her work.

"Can we eat now?" he said, when she had secured the last bandage. He held the rabbit and a knife toward her.

"Can you skin this thing and make the fire?" he asked. "And cook it?"

She smiled brightly and took both objects from him.

———

Joe pretended he wasn't that hungry, accepting only a small bite at Luz's insistence, but let her devour the rabbit.

They packed up to get going again, and after a few moments in the silence following her thanking him for at least the third time, he asked her:

"So after the baby, and you finish school, what are you gonna do? Like, what do you want to be when you grow up?"

Luz looked alarmed for a moment, caught off guard.

Then she relaxed.

"Oh, I don't know." She was quiet for a few seconds. "A nurse, I guess. Yeah, that's it."

"When did you know you wanted to be a nurse?"

"I guess since I was really young. I've always wanted to help people, and I think a nurse would be a good fit—it just occurred to me, actually. I wouldn't be a doctor or anything like that—I don't think I get good enough grades —too distracted. Anyway, I know more people who can make it through nursing school than medical school, you know?"

"Yeah." Then he said, "Do you see yourself getting married and...well, having more kids someday?"

"Oh, for sure. With a guy who's good to me, kind, will be a good father, supporter and provider—you know, all that stuff. What about you? What are you planning for your life?"

Joe shrugged. "I haven't really thought about it like that. You know how when you're a kid, like five or something, and someone ask you what you want to be? And kids always say a teacher, or fireman, or police officer—stuff like that? Well, I said all of those at some point. I'm all right in school, but I haven't been thinking about it much. And anyway, I'm only thirteen."

"You see yourself going to college?"

Joe shook his head. "College costs a lot of money we don't have."

"What about marriage and kids someday?"

"Oh yeah—now that I could see. I'd love it—to have a wife and some babies. No more than two, though—I don't think I could deal with more than that—especially if they're anything like us out here."

Luz laughed.

He smiled, enjoying seeing her lighthearted. "See, if I get to that point where I have people counting on me like that, no doubt I'll find something to do, some way of supporting them."

Then a flash of a face came to his mind and excitement

surged through him as he remembered an evening he was allowed to watch a fight with a group of friends.

"MMA!" he said as the bulb lit. "Now *that* I wouldn't mind checking out. I'd love to try it."

"So you like those dangerous occupations where you could get brain damage and shit, huh?"

"Well, you asked, so there you go—that's what appeals to me. For now anyway. Don't think I'll be a chef, I can tell you that."

He watched her giggle again, feeling warm inside.

———

"WE'RE ALMOST THERE, I know it," Joe said.

"I can't wait," Luz replied, looking down. "How many of us do you think are left?"

"Well, I hope the rest survived this far too. Everyone should get a second chance, and it would be a real shame if they didn't get one."

"We might not get one either."

"Come on, Luz..."

"I'm just being real. In any case, whether we get out of this alive or not, I want you to know I feel lucky I met you. You're a really nice guy."

Then she leaned forward and gave him a peck on the lips.

Joe couldn't believe his luck.

He thought of nothing else for the next few minutes, and had no idea how long they had been walking afterward until suddenly, Luz inhaled sharply, then grabbed onto his arm. He soon saw why.

What had initially appeared to be an odd animal clearly became two as a bobcat turned, looked at them, then ran away, leaving behind a blackened thing it had been sniffing in curiosity; in fact the entire area was charred—even the rocks—in a sort of blackened circle.

"What the hell is that?" Luz asked. "A burnt tree stump?"

Joe put his arm in front of her chest to halt her progress, silently communicating that she stay behind as he checked the object out. But as he got closer and closer to the burnt object, it became clear that it wasn't a tree stump at all, but a body that had inexplicably stayed seated while it burned, sitting upright and cross-legged, charred face split by a macabre grin, one eyeball tinged with blue staring ahead.

Luz was gagging. "God, the smell—I'm going back over there," she said, moving even further away before she got a chance to see what he had seen. And he was glad—so very glad, because there was no way she would be able to handle the object's true identity.

Joe ran back in her direction.

"What was it, Joe? A burnt baby bear or something? It looked like the remains of an animal."

Ralph, Joe responded silently. He knew by the tuft of red hair still on a partial scalp. Instead, he said: "I think so. I couldn't really handle being around it myself. Let's go the other way; we'll get around it."

All the while they trekked on, Joe wondered how Ralph had gone from traveling with who might have been the most capable, prepared member of their group, with all his proclaimed knowledge of the forest and maps and instruments, to being left behind, burned to death. He knew there was no way Ralph would have deliberately burned himself, but how had he managed to accidentally do it? Had he actually tried to protect himself by surrounding himself with fire at some point?

Nobody was that dumb.

SIXTEEN

HIGH ON THE HOG

Narine's first thought as she came to rest was that she was alive—she had somehow survived her fall down the embankment.

Then she touched her swollen, busted lips, ran her tongue over her teeth trying to find all of them, then realized she had been tasting blood.

She wondered how far she had fallen, but it was difficult to tell—her vision had a blurred quality to it.

She closed one eye, then the other and realized she had lost a contact.

Luckily, it was just one—she was near sighted so the one helped her out a bit in the daytime, but she knew it wouldn't be much help at night.

She lay there a while, momentarily frozen in fear, wondering how much time had passed, and if the monster pig would at any moment try to come after her. Then she figured it was unlikely—no creature in its right mind with that kind of mass would try to brave the incline of the embankment just for a chase. She hoped.

She found it remarkable that the first thing she thought of hadn't been her face, whether her lip gloss was still on. And even now her face wasn't her greatest concern—her thoughts went to Bluto as she wondered where he was and if he, too, had made it, despite the screaming she had heard, the damage he must've endured. Then, she thought about what a traitor he was, and if the pig had gotten him, she was glad.

But although he had thrown her to the animal, she felt sad for the boy whose sister would no longer have her protector, the brother who could no longer make good on his promise.

And then she thought—fuck it; served him right.

All for one and one for me—the only way I can survive this thing is to not depend on anyone for anything. Somehow, I'll get my own food, my own water, and I'll find a way to defeat this pig if I have to. I will get out of here!

Besides, she knew when she got back home, she would get to fix whatever was wrong with her.

Narine touched her cheek, her forehead; gently inspected her face with her hand.

She was glad she didn't have access to a mirror—she

wouldn't be able to stand looking at herself right now. She had felt at least two teeth missing, and who knew how serious her cuts and gashes were?

She wondered—would there be scarring? Who would go out with her now? Would plastic surgery and a good dentist fix everything? And if they didn't, how would she be able to get what she wanted?

She thought about what her mother would say if she could see her now. The old cow would probably laugh, for once being able to say she was more attractive than her daughter.

You shouldn't be so vain, darling, her mother had said to her once. *This*—and she and made a sweeping motion across her body—*will pass. Things will sag, dry out, wrinkle. And no one will want you.*

Like you? Narine had said carelessly in response, and she almost felt sorry immediately—those older black eyes with the wrinkles at the corner became filmy; the woman had not tried to hide her hurt in the least. Narine knew she had a knack for aiming a dagger at the right place, and she had nailed it this time around.

Daughter, it's okay if you find me plain, but listen to me when I tell you that your looks will fade, and you will find yourself all alone if you continue on this path. It doesn't take much for a man to tire of you if you are just a toy to him. Think how quickly children tire of toys and want new ones—no matter how wonderful they think the new thing is at first. Baby, I don't want this to happen to you—I don't want you to sell everything you have, everything you are, so early. You will regret it, I promise you. Men move on quickly to a shiny new thing, even before your looks start to fade.

What do you know of men, mom? You can hardly keep dad interested.

Remembering the words now sent a pain through her that she thought at first might have come from injuries related to her recent drop.

I used to be beautiful like you once, daughter.

Narine had scoffed.

It's true. Your father fell hard for me. I was twenty-three, young, energetic, full of life and myself. Nothing could stop me. The world was mine.

It was my hair he said he was crazy about, her mom had said. Thick waves, glossy black hair he'd say he just wanted to run his hands through forever. He couldn't get enough of me.

Um, eww, Narine had responded.

Daughter, don't pretend you don't know. He spoke all the right words to me and I married him. Next thing I knew, I had you. He loved you, daughter, but he eventually stopped seeing me. I don't know when it started, but he began an affair with someone in his office. I'm not sure how many there have been since, but I made this bed, and I am *lying in it. Once you are old enough, I hope I find the strength to get out of here—out of his way, and mine.*

Narine thought it was the lamest story, and as soon as there was an opening—thankfully, the ringing of her cell phone—she took it.

Thanks, mom, 'preciate it, she said, shooing her out of her room to gossip with her friend.

Her mom left quietly, head up, eyes slightly down as usual, and Narine stared at the complicated bun her hair was twisted in, wondering for the first time what her mother's hair would look like down.

Narine let out a heavy breath.

She knew Bluto was dead and she would be too if she didn't get out of the wilderness soon.

As she started limping along, thoughts of her mother continued to plague her.

She began to think maybe she would be nicer to her mom once she got back—the woman hadn't really done anything to her, and just looked so disappointed in her sometimes. Other times she looked proud—like when she introduced her to her friends. Her mom's friends would always look surprised, their eyes widening in amazement— no doubt shocked that a girl so beautiful could have come from her.

She's so grown! They would say, instead of what they probably really wanted to say, like: *She's so gorgeous!*

If her mom could only see her now. Would she be

glad? Secretly happy her beautiful child was finally ugly, and posed no threat to her? Would she be embarrassed at having such a busted daughter? Would she keep her hidden away until her scars healed, and she looked beautiful again?

Narine realized it didn't matter, really—she had walked a minute in her shoes and already felt for the woman slowly fading away in front of everyone's eyes.

She couldn't imagine what it felt like for people like her mom who walked around almost invisible. There were several girls in school like that—she could barely recall their faces.

Narine always thought how annoying it was that she could hardly go anywhere without being noticed, being propositioned. Having guys see her as a piece of meat they wanted to take a bite of, and felt they deserved a shot at. All the work she put in got recognized, but she got ticked at the various losers she didn't do all the work for. If only they could just disappear and realize how unworthy they were, how little they had to offer.

Narine sometimes resented she couldn't sneak anywhere to do anything—always too conspicuous, too noticeable. She got frustrated by the lack of privacy sometimes, and had even wished for a dash of what invisible people went through now and then, but as she thought about it now, invisibility was probably ten times worse than its opposite. To walk around feeling like no one thought anything of you, that nothing about you was valuable at first glance. To have to work hard to get store clerks to come over and pay attention—she saw it happen to people all the time.

Narine couldn't imagine not getting the smiles she constantly received from random strangers—male and female—just because they liked looking at her. For everything, people were more forgiving, more accommodating. Men opened doors for her, women asked her about her secrets—makeup tricks, skin potions, exercise regime. She got in places without tickets, past doormen without being carded, without having to wait in line. Service was always with a smile unless she encountered some jealous bitch—male or female—whose bitterness was eating her up looking at all the things she wasn't and wanted to be in front of her.

People tried to strike up conversations with her for no good reason—in the cashier's line at a store, while she sat on a bench texting, while washing her hands in a damned public restroom. No rest, no reprieve for the pretty.

But it was definitely, decidedly better than the alternative.

As she walked on, the details of the wilderness distracted her from her thoughts now that it was not only daytime, but she was also alone, not being sucked into some lame conversation or forced to lead one.

She saw a different type of beauty around her—the

shade of the sky, the greens around her—hues MAC couldn't touch.

She heard what seemed like a chorus at certain times of the day. She wasn't sure what creatures were involved, but she figured insects and frogs were behind the songs. She wished she could see them, but most times she was content to just hear their music.

She paused to watch butterflies gracefully land on this tree, that flower, this blade of grass. A rust-colored salamander wiggling into a log, bright-colored mushrooms peeking out from moss and brush, some cream-colored, some red and white. Birds of many types flying above, doing an interpretive sky dance, making formations, chirping amongst branches. Fowl she had no idea of their names—blue ones and brown ones and black ones. All aware of her, but not startled, not bothered in the least, it seemed. As if it were all...natural. Like she belonged here with all these different types of living things.

Surely they were simply used to humans, but to feel so accepted by creatures who varied so widely and had never met her before, yet allowed her in their space without suspicion gave her inexplicable joy.

And as much as she wanted to go home to her familiar room—lilac walls, lilac and white bedspread on her full bed, warm and dry, parents just down the hall, food readily available in the fridge, shower just a few feet away with bath salts, body wash, soap, loofah, lotions and perfumes, cosmetics and pretty clothing nearby—this too, with all its rugged terrain and sometimes foul smells, sometimes pine smells, scarce food and sense of danger, and the rest of its unknown factors—felt like home.

SEVENTEEN

HOGTIED

"Davdi!"

David went on the defense instantly, drawing a knife as soon as he heard his name—despite the fact that it had been shouted almost ecstatically in a feminine voice. He turned toward the sound and saw someone running toward him with what he figured was supposed to be a smile.

Then he recognized the awful shirt.

He knew exactly who it was, but still asked:

"Who the fuck are you?"

The busted creature promptly halted her joyous run toward him as he stood in a defensive stance, weapon still drawn.

The clumsy smile slowly disappeared. "It's me!" it said, "Narine!"

David relaxed and put his weapon away. "I thought

you were a wild hillbilly. What the hell happened to you? Looks like that beast got you, but you managed to slip away just before it mauled you to death. Christ."

Narine managed to look hurt. "Is it really that bad?" she asked.

He nodded. "Horrible."

She sighed and put her hand through her hair, but it got stuck. She worked it free.

"Anyway, I can't worry about that now. I've got to focus on the most important thing, which is getting the fuck out of here alive. I can fix things when I get out. My dad will help me fix things."

David was amused by her self pep-talk. "I'm sure he will, princess."

Narine gave him a look.

"You know, you're kind of freaking me out with your eyes," he said. "I mean, I knew the color wasn't real, but the way you look right now with your hair all crazy—shit stuck in it, all tangled and leafy with some blood sticking some of it together—teeth missing, black and blue bruises, but on top of all that, one blue eye and one dark eye? You'd pull a knife on you too."

"Way to lay it on thick, David."

"You look like some mad bush woman, like you belong here. Why do you even bother wearing blue contacts anyway? You know you're not fooling anyone."

She shrugged. "People find it prettier, whether they think it's real or not."

"I don't know—I find it about as attractive as a man dressed as a woman with his balls hanging out of his mini skirt; just can't buy it."

"Well, plenty of men can, and do. But that's right; you're not a man, are you?"

David laughed. "It's you after all, Narine!"

"Look, I'm sorry, but can you just lay off my looks for a second? It's literally the least important thing right now with what's going on. Like, literally. I mean, we're trying to stay alive and get out of here. We need to make sure we can take care of the basics like food and water. Anyway, how come this is as far as you've got? Is your sense of direction really that bad?"

She gave a grin he knew would've looked bitchy cute before, but now just looked homeless pathetic.

"I'm making my way. And I'm doing something right— I'm still alive, ain't I?"

"That's true, but where's Ralph, then? Didn't you guys go off together? What happened to him? Is he peeing or something right now?" She looked around.

David affected a disappointed stance, dropping his shoulders and looking down.

He realized then they were walking in step together and admired her ability to keep up—or perhaps he had slowed down to accommodate her without realizing it.

"Nah—Ralph didn't make it. We had a face-off with the pig, and I got away, but...well, he didn't."

One scratched hand came to her chest and he noticed her chipped nails. "Oh my god—that's terrible! I was lucky, I guess. How did you get away? And what did the creature look like?"

"Oh, it was horrible—scariest thing I've ever seen in my life. Huge, smelled weird, made all these horrible noises. It was dark grey with bristly hair and insects attached to it and, oh boy, those tusks. I got up a tree right away and Ralph was a little too slow on the draw. He was an easier, smaller target anyway, I guess." David shook his head—reverently, he hoped. "It was awful seeing him gored like that right below me, hearing him cry out, scream for his life. That beast was relentless."

He thought he saw Narine quickly look around before asking her next question. "So when did you come down? How long were you up there?"

"Shit, I don't know—I stayed up there till it was gone. It didn't look like it cared to wait for me, but just to be sure, I watched it leave the area, climbed higher and saw bushes and stuff parting where it passed through. It really seemed to go on its merry way, but still, I watched for a while. The good news is, a thing like that doesn't come quietly—there's quite a bit of noise for warning."

"Too bad it could almost be any creature out here and have you on edge for nothing."

"Yeah, but it makes a piggy sound, you know? A kind of snorty snort. Anyway, I got high enough in the tree where I got an idea what other kinds of trees were around that I could scale if needed. You sure can see a lot from up there."

"So you had to come down and pass Ralph's body? God, eww—how horrific. Well, the pig obviously has no problem attacking people in twos. I guess when you're a big creature like that, two measly kids don't mean squat. I'm glad I didn't see Bluto's body, even though he betrayed me like that."

"What do you mean?"

"When the pig came after us and it came down to it, Bluto tripped me once we started running so it would get me first. But that's how I ended up like this." She pointed to her face. "When he tripped me, I didn't just fall—I ended up rolling down this hill. I must've hit everything on the way down."

"Yup, sure looks like it."

She was quiet for a few seconds. "Ironically, he ended up saving me for sure. I don't know if I would've been able to outrun him, or if that would have even mattered if the beast had just chosen me for whatever reason, 'cause I sure as hell couldn't outrun that thing."

"Yeah, they're quick," David agreed.

"I probably shouldn't even be walking with you, but boy am I glad to see you. Anyone, really—I've been walking by myself for a while. And it'll be good to have some company at night if we're still here for any reason—someone to help me stay awake and all that. You know —'two heads are better than one.' Four pairs of eyes, two sets of defenses..."

"Your face might be a defense, love."

"Cut it out, David, please?"

David laughed. "I knew it—you can dish it, but you can't take it, can you, sweetheart? Just like everyone else. You make everything about your looks, shit's always gonna be about your looks."

"Yeah, whatever. So I was an asshole. I'll probably still be one after I get my face fixed. The gashes and bruises will heal, and a plastic surgeon can take care of any scars. I can easily get my teeth sorted out and look even better than before. I can still be pretty."

"Who are you trying to convince? Do you have to say that to yourself every half hour or so?"

"Look, how about we start talking about your strategy for getting out of here? Which direction were you heading? I need to know. I like having a partner, but not one who I think is going the wrong way."

"Well, I was planning to head through those trees over there," he said, pointing away from the sun.

"Okay, that seems about right—that's where I was headed anyway. Did you plan on setting up camp tonight? Or powering through?"

"Probably set up camp, save some energy. I think fire might help keep it away."

Narine's broken smile appeared. "Me too."

And he smiled back at her. But not for the same reason she smiled at him, he was sure; in fact, she would sprint away in horror if she had an inkling of his thoughts.

One indeed saw a lot from the trees, like an unaware beast busting through the forest toward two hapless teens, intent clear.

Luckily, David had a prime viewing vantage point, and was able to make out Bluto's last desperate attempt to remain alive, hoping to shove his hiking partner in the way of the beast instead. But he had only made it easier for the beast to choose who would be its first victim.

David watched Bluto clumsily try to scale a tree, and that beautiful, sweet moment when he finally found himself face to face with the monster. David couldn't see the horror or surprise on Bluto's face, and for that, he was sad. He would have liked to see the sheer terror as the creature started ripping him to pieces. Still, he got to see Bluto's blood splatter as the monster gored him relentlessly.

Most of what he had described to Narine came from witnessing Bluto's demise, and it appeared to him she had swallowed his story hook, line, and sinker. But then again, what choice did she have? She had no reason to believe he would lie to her.

Besides, she had missed the entire episode as she tumbled down the embankment. She never saw the beast, didn't get a good look at the fearless creature bent on taking them all out. She didn't see the moment when Bluto's spirit and body parted ways, or when the beast finished its task, and halted its attack. When it seemed to admire its own work.

She wasn't there when he and the beast met eye to eye as the creature sniffed him out, finally realizing it had an audience.

David knew he was a marked man, but in the lock of their eyes, he felt an understanding with the wild creature.

Then the beast took off.

There were four of them left now: him, the final hiking pair of Joe and Luz, and Narine—although not for long.

He would deal with the other pawns later; Narine was too easy a target, and he didn't mind losing this queen to the game.

———

NARINE LOOKED calm as she stared into the fire, although her mind seemed elsewhere.

"I never thought anything like this could happen out here. I don't even know what I thought—I guess that I'd learn to build fires, read maps and compasses, identify different animal tracks—things like that. Pitching tents, finding my own food—that I expected. But a chance I might not make it back alive? And now..." Her voice broke. "Now all I want is to go home. I definitely didn't expect that—to have the experience touch me like this, or this." She touched her face. "But I guess I never felt so alone, either. It's so easy to take everything for granted when you pretty much have everything, whether you know it or not."

David let out a long-held exasperated breath.

"I can't take this anymore. Enough of that, okay, Narine? Christ. I don't need to hear that 'my life has changed' shit. Seriously. Spare me your revelations—it's not that deep."

"But it is! At least for me it is. I mean, look at me. And look how many of us are left. How could anyone not be affected by any of this? I didn't know a single person who had died before! And in a matter of days, I know at least, like, four people who have gotten killed."

She let out a jagged breath, one that made him think she was holding back tears. Then she looked directly at him with her creepy, mismatched eyes. "Do you know what happened out there? When I finally came to a stop after rolling down that embankment? I don't know how long I lay there, but at some point, something came flying down the hill toward me, like a balled up animal. I watched it coming, still not sure I was alive, thinking maybe I was trapped in some strange, comatose dream since the world didn't look like I remembered it. Well, as that thing bounced and rolled toward me, it eventually came to a stop, running up against my stomach. For some crazy reason my hand went to it, and I picked it up to inspect it. I wish I could say it was an illusion from having one contact in, but I'm nearsighted, and see clearly up close. That thing was a hand—a human hand. Bluto's, probably, since he had been—or was still being—mauled up there.

"It took everything in me not to scream, but I immediately dropped the hand while holding back a shriek 'cause I knew one thing right then: I couldn't draw attention to where I was, and the fact I was still alive. Next thing you know that creature would come bounding down after me, and I didn't want to be reduced to pieces too. Anyway, when I could get myself to get up and move, I stayed low while I made my way past the site of Bluto's death so I wouldn't have to see his body. I mean, who knew what other pieces had come off? Besides, he and I actually had some fun together, and although he betrayed me, I was still sad about him getting killed like that. I learned so much about him—about his dad, his sister, other things about his life. He had all these plans and wanted to make sure he got back to protect his sister, and now she's gonna be in foster care by herself and..." She burst into tears.

David watched her for a few seconds. "I can't travel with you like this," he said. "You're a liability."

She stopped crying immediately. "Well, what do you

expect me to do? I'm not completely heartless, you know! I'd be sad if you died too."

"Look, you need to keep your head on. Keeping your shit together is one of the only ways we'll get out of this. Mourn later."

She wiped away a tear with a crude swipe of her arm. "You're a weirdo," she said. "Like, do you feel anything? How could you not be upset about any of this?"

"Because I can't afford to," he said simply. "You know how to compartmentalize, don't you? Well, expand your abilities. Nothing cares about you or your pussy here; no one's going to give you anything for it. Look at Bluto even. He was willing to take care of you in exchange for it, but what did even he do in the end? That's right. Trust no one but yourself."

"But I think we can trust each other sometimes."

"I think that's a mistake."

"You can trust me," she said, and he knew the dumb girl meant it.

———

It registered to Narine that she had gone more than twenty-four hours without real sleep.

Fatigue hit her like an outstretched branch while rolling helplessly down a hill. She didn't even know when she had dozed off.

She remembered watching the fire, David setting up a tent, sending her to lie down inside. He had said something about keeping watch.

She had only meant to close her eyes for a few minutes, but it was as if weights were attached to her eyelids.

The silence eventually woke her—she suddenly felt alone. She opened her eyes and listened. Nothing in particular sounded out of order, but she knew something was wrong.

She sat up, listening.

Then she peeked out of the tent and looked around.

David was nowhere in sight.

"David?" she called out.

Perhaps he was taking a potty break.

She climbed out of the tent, listening carefully.

"David?" she called again.

She looked around for his stuff, any sign that he might have actually left her behind for good. His blanket was there at least, and her own backpack still right outside the tent.

She relaxed.

She started to move closer to the fire when she heard something move in the bushes.

"David?" she called hopefully.

But the sound was not at all like a teenage boy casually strolling back to the site.

She began to panic, wondering what she could use in her backpack as a weapon. It could've been anything coming toward her, even a bear. She preferred a bear, considering what she had heard about that horrible pig; she didn't want to get more damaged in battle, didn't want to think about getting torn up and gashed by a vicious animal. She didn't want to lose another nail much less a finger.

Besides, she could handle a bear—the camp leader had mentioned a few defenses: roll into a ball, just lay still. Play dead. Or hold your arms above your head so you seem larger, while backing away slowly. But never run. And climbing up a tree may or may not help, depending on the bear.

Still, she looked around quickly for a viable tree and caught a glimpse of something that pricked her interest, but didn't have time to investigate as a wild animal finally broke through the forest and came toward her snorting and chomping.

She was momentarily confused; it was not a bear at all.

She heard a horrible squeal before the impact, and her flesh was broken once, twice, three times, pain ripping through her as she fruitlessly tried to twist away.

As the animal knocked her down and continued to gore her, she finally had the vantage point to understand what had caught her eyes earlier in the trees.

It was a human face, barely illuminated by the small

glowing fire below. A round face with shark eyes, and, oddly enough, a smile.

Why would David be smiling at a moment like this?

Her vision blurred and everything began to dim.

She welcomed the numbness coming over her body, beginning to beat out the sharp stabs of pain, and conjured up an image of her mom—the younger face she had seen in an old photo.

"I'm sorry," she said to the image, and she imagined the image folding her into a warm hug.

EIGHTEEN

THIS LITTLE PIGGY WENT TO MARKET

David had watched mushrooms magically turn a human brain into a confused, waterlogged machine, then destroy itself from the outside in by fire.

Manipulating people's actions and thoughts had almost become too easy; people were so much more vulnerable and susceptible to suggestion than they would ever admit to. It almost started to bore him—a kid like Ralph had worn his desire to be accepted on his sleeve.

Odds were against Ralph to begin with—a small, myopic thing whose skin the sun ridiculed. A boy like that couldn't even risk being outside in his own world too long in the daytime. Maybe that's why he liked lighting the night.

David knew it was safe to confess to Ralph as he sat there in his circle of fire, like some Buddhist monk or confessional priest.

"I fucked up," he said to an oblivious Ralph. "With my dad. I lost it; I might have killed him. The problem is, I *am* defective; I am a monster, Ralph, and there's no going back."

Now David watched Narine die, her body beyond repair at last as the creature took no mercy on her face, her beautiful breasts, her legs. It seemed to take great pleasure in tearing up the human body, as if trained to maim, kill, damage irreversibly. To shame and embarrass a corpse beyond vanity.

Then the creature, having satisfied its bloodlust, took off, not even seeking his eyes this time, although David was almost sure it was aware of him.

As for Narine—she would probably be glad she was no longer recognizable in the least. That perhaps only a coroner and her parents would get to see her tattered body when she was blue and far beyond care; that is, if other wild animals didn't get to her first, tearing her apart further; ingesting her, using her for their own survival, then pooping her out around the forest.

David stayed in the tree until light came, knowing the animal was nowhere around, and didn't have his sights set on him just yet.

He took one last look at Narine's torn, bloodstained corpse, then like his favorite chess piece, he just up and left.

Up and left.

DAVID'S WORK was almost done: all he had to do now was lead the creature to the last two pawns—one final misdirection.

Finding Luz and Joe's trail was beyond easy. He wondered if they were just that stupid and careless, or that clueless about how easy they made it to be tracked by any animal.

Sure, they probably had other things on their minds, and wouldn't know they were the last ones left, but didn't they know how urgent it was that they find smarter ways to maneuver their way out of the forest?

Maybe they just didn't know the murderous creature could track their human trail, or thought they were close enough to think they were in the clear. Maybe they had already given up and decided to go as far as they could, come what may.

Maybe they were too tired and hungry, so they were delusional and sloppy.

In any case, David was both happy and disappointed they had made it so easy for him to find them, and bring them all together.

Things David wished he had: more pawns to play with.

No one had died around Joe and Luz in a while. They had been free from screams of terror and torture for one whole day, allowing internal thoughts to dominate, the space between the silence to get filled.

Then, a voice came to Joe, nudged him in the shoulder with its tiny pitchfork; a miniature devil wearing a halo whispering: *Tell her. You can take care of her. One of your aunts lives in Cali—maybe she'll let you stay there. Just tell her, Joe, tell her!*

"Luz, I..."

"Don't, Joe," she said to his surprise. She couldn't possibly know what he was about to say?

"I think I love you, Luz," he still blurted out.

Luz chuckled, and it saddened him. "No, you don't," she said.

"I've never felt this way before! Fine, laugh. I really like you, then—how about that?"

"I'll accept that. But it's only because we're trapped in this horrible situation."

He shook his vigorously. "No. Since the first time I saw you...I don't know what it was. I didn't even know you were pregnant then, or anything about you. But I think I loved you from then."

She was still smiling, but there was a hint of bitterness to it. "You're cute," she said, and the way she said it almost made him mad.

It was kind of condescending, that's what it was. Did she think he was too young for her? Was he still considered a little boy? She was only one year older! And he no longer doubted he was a man. "Why don't you believe me?"

"I don't know if love works like that, Joe, honestly. But maybe...maybe I love you too. You're probably the best guy I ever met. If we survive, though, it's probably all over, right? I mean, I've got a kid coming, Joe. I don't even know where you live, but I know it's not near San Diego. Our families...shit, it wouldn't work. If grandma didn't accept Emilio, I'm pretty sure she won't accept you."

"But why?"

She refused to answer. Her mouth had completely turned up in bitterness. "We're kids," she said finally, looking away. "Anything we have right now is a joke."

Her words shattered his heart.

He hadn't realized he had been staring at the ground until she turned to him and tilted his head back up with one of her fingers.

She looked into his eyes. "I'm sorry," she said. "I just don't know where this is going. Where anything is going. I don't need you confusing things, confusing me. I'm sorry," she said again.

After some moments passed, she said:

"But Joe, I would name the baby Joseph if it's a boy. Like you."

Joe felt his heart repairing, swelling with a pride he had never felt, and for the first time, he believed his grandmother: Joe is going to make something of himself.

———————

DAVID HAD HEARD and seen enough.

He knew the beast was coming, and through his many observations of Joe and Luz, realized Joe might get in the way of his goal: a stalemate. To take Joe on would have presented an interesting challenge, but it was best to get the pair out of the wild, have them distract the outside with their tales of forest monsters, while he disappeared into the wilderness.

He had never pulled the trigger before, but he had to kill the beast.

David looked at the yellow unit in his hand one more time, sent the SOS signal, then tossed it—along with a flare gun—ahead of the couple, stopping them in their tracks.

Luz immediately picked up the items, while Joe went on guard, looking around him while in a defensive stance.

Then they scanned the area with their eyes, no doubt trying to identify the source of the unexpected bounty, but David knew they would never locate him. They, however, would easily be found.

They would discover the SOS button on the personal

locator beacon and send another signal, and rescuers would be on the way soon.

David ignored their shouts into the wilderness, their requests for identification, that he come forward.

He knew what would happen if he did, could see quite clearly in his mind's eye how that move would play out.

David! They would both say in surprise, and probably delight. Then they would insist he join them.

But he couldn't go back where he would be a monster.

What? You're not a monster, David—we all did bad things, but we're not all monsters, Luz would probably say if she got an inkling of his thoughts. Then again, if she knew his thoughts, perhaps she would agree with him.

David smiled to himself.

He watched Joe and Luz struggle with their decision to eventually keep moving, then settle at the base of a tree to wait for first responders.

You don't belong here, but I do, he said silently to the oblivious couple. *There's no going back.*

He had to help Nathan Colt track down the beast and end the game.

———

"If we make it back okay, you think you'd still give the baby up?" Joe asked Luz, breaking their most recent heavy silence as they sat against a tree, backpacks beside them.

Luz smiled at him, feeling a welcome warmth for both the smitten boy and the life in her belly.

"I think I've changed my mind, actually. I'm keeping...him," she said. "He and I can make it. Heck, if I can make it through this, we can make it through anything." She rested her hand on her belly, to assure the little one within.

"Will you keep in touch with me?" Joe asked with such hope in his eyes, there was no denying him.

"Of course! How could we not at least stay friends after all this?"

"I'd like to meet him...or her," Joe said shyly.

"You're welcome to," she replied, meaning every word. Then she reached out and touched his hand softly, gently. "I'd love for you to be in our lives, Joe. We'll make it happen."

The smile that broke out on Joe's face could've lit a moonless night.

What interrupted the moment was the sound of something so alien to the forest, so outside of their world for the past few days, that it took them both a few seconds to recognize it. Then they looked up for the source.

"That's for us!" Luz yelled, ecstatic.

She recognized the faint sound of blades pounding the air—a helicopter sent to rescue them, surely. They were safe, and would be back home with their families in no time, out of this hellhole of death and danger.

Joe began fumbling with the flare gun.

But soon, they heard a rush through the forest.

They both looked at each other, knowing immediately something was on the way—there was no mistaking the galloping sound of a charging animal.

Joe helped Luz up the tree, then quickly climbed up after her. They made their way up the next branch, out of reach of what was likely the bloodthirsty monster headed their way.

The thicket of green leaves and brittle branches seemed to roll toward them powerfully, turning and twisting. Then it abruptly ceased, and another movement caught their focus—this one, a man galloping toward them, occasionally hopping above the sea of plants to plead for their attention. Soon, he too was lost in the layered foliage.

Luz held on to Joe firmly.

Then, just feet behind the clearing surrounding them, they heard a heavy, forceful breath, filling Luz with dread.

Soon, the creature charged ahead, but instead of a gigantic, nasty grey beast bursting through the bushes, out tumbled Nathan Colt, the odd man from the first night.

It seemed the wild had devastated him, his body now caked in blood-red mud, barely recognizable. A thousand tiny lashes on his skin oozed and trickled blood around the moss and plant bits that seemed splattered against his face and arms.

He collapsed at the foot of their tree, gasping for breath.

"Help me," he said, with his head down. Then he painstakingly raised himself up and looked at them directly. "Help me!" he repeated, lifting his arms toward them. "It's coming after me, help me up! I can't climb—I'm broken with this leg."

Joe only stared at Nate, while holding on to Luz tightly.

His look was cold.

"It won't hold," he said, amazing Luz with how firm and hard his usually soft-edged voice had become.

She imagined the tree was plenty strong for all of them, but she trusted Joe.

Luz looked from one man to the next. Then she fixed her eyes on the forest behind Nate, and saw no signs of another large animal.

"I'm protecting her," Joe said gently but firmly.

He didn't take his eyes off of Nate's.

Nate looked shocked and his fingers still pleaded, wiggling for a few seconds as if they could magically summon helping hands, before he brought his arms back down.

His look spoke words to Joe that Luz didn't quite catch. Comprehension, and something like respect bathed his face with still a hint of a question, mouth hanging slightly open before it closed and tightened.

Nate no longer looked afraid of a monster behind him, completely in the moment of what had transpired between him and Joe.

Suddenly, Nathan Colt slammed his teeth together. With violent power, he snarled, continuing to bash his teeth, never breaking his gaze with Joe. He added first the slamming and thrashing of his prosthetic war trophy into the ground, then pulled two blood-soaked blades from behind his back and added them to the rhythmic cacophony.

The fear that raced through Luz was matched only by the awe she felt faced with such a beast. He was a mass of pulsating muscle and rage, an irreverent force, and it seemed he was trying to smash himself to pieces.

Blood dripping from his teeth, Nate let his spit and tears fly freely during his dance.

Then the song stopped, and the man who was Nathan Colt cried out with such unrestrained force that his voice cracked, twisted, and squealed—an animalistic sound that rippled through Luz, standing her body hairs on end.

Luz finally put two and two together.

She grabbed the flare gun from Joe and shot into the sky, the simple red flame briefly dividing it.

The beast thrashed as he circled them, and Luz wondered for a frightened moment if it would use its weapons to help it ascend the tree.

Then Joe said:

"The whole world is coming, Nate," and as if on cue, the helicopter returned, its blades suddenly louder.

The helicopter illuminated the area, and moments before an army of dancing flashlights arrived, the beast retreated into the thick to run back into the forest the way he had come, a horrible squeal lingering in the air behind him.

———

So the soldier killed the huntsman—he was
    wounded from before
From a battle with a father of the child
    splayed on the floor
And though he tried to warn the others that
    the beast was at the door
His warnings were unheeded—they carried
    on as before
Now the feral hog will kill them all unless
    they prove they're able
Kill the beast, slit his throat—leave him on
    the table.

"A man must know who he is, and where he is."
    —Enoch St. John

ABOUT THE AUTHOR

Enoch St. John has a degree in political science with a concentration in comparative politics from UCSD, as well as a degree in english literature, communication, and art.

St. John has lived in a handful of countries—a few in the West Indies—and several U. S. states, including New York, Minnesota, California, and Washington.

He is currently in southern California.

Contact:
enochstjohn@yahoo.com

ACKNOWLEDGMENTS

Ryan O' Toole

Frederik Selchau

For your honesty, insights, and time, we sincerely thank you.